Even Thistles Bloom

C.C. Hansen

Dancing Willows Press

CONTENT WARNING: This book portrays drug use, violence, and mild profanity

To everyone who has ever needed, or granted, a second chance.

"If you fell down yesterday, stand up today."

H.G. Wells

CHAPTER 1

When your mom has more boyfriends than bobby pins, you learn not to eavesdrop, but Todd doubted a conversation with his father would escalate beyond sharp words and icy glares. He shifted into a crouch on the staircase, eager ears reaching for their voices.

"I don't have the money," his father said. He meant he didn't have the money for them.

"Then you can explain to your sons why they can't play football this year."

Todd restrained a snort. As if their teammates would welcome them back after last year's debacle. He shifted farther down the staircase to catch a glimpse of his father. Todd had inherited his dad's thick blond hair and stocky build, but he didn't know whose personality he'd gotten. He hoped neither's.

"I gave you enough for football and wrestling. I have other kids to feed."

"Yes, with your lovely wife." Todd didn't need to see his mother's face to know she sneered. "You could have been my one and only, Ryan."

Todd pondered the comment, wondering what his life would be like if his parents had undergone a shotgun wedding. Would his mother be more tenderhearted if her first love hadn't ditched her? Would she have been a mom who cut the crusts off her kids' sandwiches, cheered from the bleachers, and organized fundraisers? Would his father have helped with homework, dictated chores, and roughhoused with his boys? Would they have been a stereotypical happy family with a white picket fence and a golden retriever?

1

No. Knowing his parents, they'd have divorced within a month.

"I am not responsible for the choices you made after we broke up." Ryan's words sounded as if he were reading them off the transcript of his last therapy session.

"But you are responsible for the children you made before we broke up." Todd's mother plucked at her ex's button-up shirt. He pushed her away and she laughed. "Worried I'll leave a smudge for your wife to find?" Her voice turned wicked. "You haven't confessed your past mistakes, have you? Shall I call her? I gave the boys your last name. She'll probably believe me even before seeing the paternity test results."

Ryan's square jaw tensed, hard as a cinderblock. "You've had seventeen years to find your own happiness. Don't take mine just because you can't handle failure."

"Who said I'm unhappy?" She leaned casually against the railing, and Todd scooted farther up the staircase to avoid being seen. "I'm a modern woman, liberated to be with whomever I want, whenever I want."

"Is that what you tell yourself?"

"Just get me the money."

Todd's father must have nodded, because the door slammed and a car started. His mother took a phone call in the next room. Her wheedling had developed recently, no doubt brought on by her aging into the wrong half of thirty for a woman in her profession. She, of course, called herself an "interior design consultant," but as far as Todd knew, her only income derived from sleeping with rich men.

Todd trudged to the room he shared with his twin, Adam, who lounged in bed, still in his pajamas.

"How is dear old Dad?" Adam said without looking up from his phone.

Todd slumped into his desk chair. "The usual."

"Why do you even bother?"

Todd couldn't answer. Adam had given up wishing their father would rescue them from their mother's custody, but Todd had never fully squashed the hope that dwelled in his belly. It should've died after his father married, but hope was a stubborn parasite, squirming every time his father sent them a birthday card or attended a football game. Todd imagined it would dance a jig if his father ever talked to him instead of lurking in the periphery of his life.

Todd fired up his laptop and entered the now-familiar search terms, his typing hampered by the four short stumps that remained of his left fingers. The injury hindered him little, but he loathed the ever-present reminder of a night he'd rather forget.

The search engine summoned the photograph of his father standing with his arm around Shanice. The younger woman had deep brown skin and a snubby nose that said she wouldn't approve of her husband's "mistakes" even if he had the balls to confess. In front of them stood two elementary-aged children—a girl and a boy. *I bet they have a picket fence and a retriever.*

How had those kids earned their father's love when Todd and Adam received rejection from day one? Todd had never longed for more siblings—a twin was enough—but as he regarded his half-siblings' smiling faces, he wondered how being a big brother would feel. Adam never let him forget their ten-minute age difference—always dragging him into trouble, weaseling out of said trouble, and setting up dubious double dates. What would it be like to show a younger kid how to survive school?

The thought descended through a dark spiral. Todd wasn't a role model any sane mother would want for their children. Shanice would be right to snub him if they ever met.

"Can I have a copy?"

Todd jumped. He hadn't noticed his brother move to peer over his shoulder. "Why?"

"It's the closest we'll ever get to a family reunion, right?" Adam said, but his mischievous grin hinted at devious plans for the photo.

Todd printed the picture, hoping his brother's scheme died before coming to fruition. He couldn't afford a repeat of last year.

"I'm heading next door," Todd said as he handed Adam the printout.

"We have—"

"I know. I'll be back in time."

Todd trudged downstairs and out the door, enjoying the late summer sunshine on his face as he traversed the lot to his neighbors' garden center. The familiar smells of warm mulch, fragrant flowers, and ripe fertilizer hit Todd as he entered the building. Mrs. Thompson sat at the register, typing with fingers much paler than a gardener's should be. She looked older than her fifty-seven years, the result of some muscular disease Todd couldn't spell. As her condition worsened, she spent more time in her recliner while her son ran the place. Today must be a good day.

"Good afternoon, Todd." Disappointment tinged her greeting, as if she blamed herself for how he'd turned out. Todd and his brother had spent most of their childhood in her care. "Noah is in the greenhouse. I'm sure he has a to-do list for you."

After years assisting the family, Todd didn't need a list, but he nodded before entering the muggy greenhouse. Noah, Mrs. Thompson's son, lifted a planter to the hanging chain, his squat body making the task difficult. Once he'd secured the planter, he turned his flat-featured face toward Todd.

"Can you water rows three through five?" He misarticulated the words, but Todd had known him long enough to understand. He grabbed a hose and began spraying the plants with warm water.

Todd had always known Noah was "different," but it was Adam who'd discovered they could outsmart him. Many harshly punished practical jokes later, Mrs. Thompson's disease set in. Being able to outrun the mom and outsmart the son meant Adam no longer felt beholden to the pair's commands, but Todd continued to come here. He made pennies per hour, but Mrs. Thompson fed him if he helped, which was better pay than gold by Todd's reckoning. Besides, he couldn't resist the greenery. Plants were never disappointed to see him.

He watered a row of marigolds, whose yellow blooms accepted the offering cheerfully. Something wet nudged the back of his calf. Todd flicked off the hose and turned to find Fifi, Noah's one-eyed three-legged terrier, begging for attention. He scratched behind the rescue dog's ears, knowing Noah didn't care how long he took to water the plants as long as they didn't go thirsty.

He finished watering the rows, then swept the floor and restacked a set of pots that a customer had left askew. By the end of the morning, his body hummed, satisfied from the hard day's work. Without sports, manual labor provided his only route to that contentment. At school, he suffered lectures from burned out teachers, fought with cranky classmates, and struggled through homework beyond his capabilities. At home, he tuned out his mother's shrieking demands, followed Adam's crazy schemes, and smoked as much weed as possible. Getting high dulled his senses, but the muggy greenhouse air transported him to another world. Here with Noah and Fifi, he didn't need to smoke to forget his troubles.

As if summoned by the thought, Noah appeared beside him. He grinned and thrust a marigold plant into Todd's hands.

"Summer bonus. Too many to sell before winter." Winter meant replacing the delicate flowers with hardy vegetables.

"Thanks, but..." Todd didn't want to hurt Noah's feelings, but he couldn't imagine the pretty bloom surviving his toxic household. He tried to return it, but Noah pushed it back into his hands.

"Keep it." He strode away before Todd could object.

Todd eyed the plant, feeling the need to apologize for what it would soon endure, but he hauled it home anyway. He set it next to his bed, chomped down a small lunch, and showered quickly, knowing he and Adam had an appointment to keep.

Adam honked as he was toweling dry. Todd joined him in the car, a gift from the only one of his mother's boyfriends who'd lasted long enough to play stepdad. Escaping their mother must have taken precedence over the vehicle, because he'd never retrieved it after they broke up.

School wouldn't start for a couple weeks, but Adam bypassed closer parking spots in favor of their usual place near the football field. Whistles from early season sports practices filled the air, and a heaviness settled on Todd's chest. He missed football. This would have been their senior year, the grand finale of high school sports. He'd been one of the league's best kickers.

Adam eschewed the main entrance and led Todd through a side door. Over a century of renovations created a maze of hallways, but Todd knew the old building well enough to realize Adam wasn't leading him to the office.

He halted as Adam leaned against the wall near the boys' locker room. A long whistle sounded, and the football players streamed in from practice. Adam, what are you thinking?

The team stopped short of him, forming a defensive line. Adam grinned.

"Hey, guys."

Jeff Chen, aka Asian Tom Brady, stepped forward. "What do you want"—he glanced at Adam's left hand—"Adam?"

Todd curled his whole fingers into a fist. Jeff had been a friend, so why couldn't he tell them apart? He forced his fingers straight. It didn't matter now.

"Come on, Jeff. You're still mad?" Adam said. "It was a joke."

Todd's stomach flipped, unsure whether Adam believed he'd win their friends back or if he was just trolling. Since he was standing by a drinking fountain—an obvious reference to the fountain he'd "prank" marked with a sign reading WHITES ONLY last year—Todd guessed the latter.

"It wasn't funny," Cumar Ahmed intoned. The levelheaded linebacker usually avoided fights in favor of helping the others keep their GPAs above the minimum, but now his dark brown eyes flashed with a threat.

Jeff pushed Adam away from the locker room entrance. "Athletes only." He disappeared inside, and the team followed, spearing Adam and Todd with angry glares. Even Ian Billings, a large but timid white guy, shook his head at them.

"Run, pansies," Adam called into the locker room. He whispered his next sentence. "We'll get you back for kicking us off the team."

Todd refrained from pointing out that the school hadn't technically barred them from trying out. Their coach had not-so-politely requested they renege in the name of "team cohesion." Exile was an apt punishment for their "prank," especially considering what followed, but Adam pined for vengeance. God, Adam, can't we move on? Todd just wanted to survive high school, and then...what? Maybe the guidance counselor will give me some career ideas.

Speaking of...

Todd checked the clock. "We're late, Adam."

Adam took off at a rage-filled pace. Todd followed, just as he always did, even if Adam leaped straight into trouble. Friends came and went like his mother's boyfriends, but Adam remained.

Todd hoped their former teammates' ire was the day's only trouble, but he tensed as soon as he reached the air-conditioned main office area. A new name graced the principal's door: CLARENCE EVANS.

The school secretary's ridiculously long fingernails clacked as she typed at her desk, which guarded the other offices like the ticket counter at a movie theater.

"We're here to see Mrs. Moore," Adam said, taking the lead as always.

The secretary's lips pursed as if they'd just added another two inches to the stack of paperwork beside her.

"Adam can go right in. Todd, wait here." She gestured to a couple of worn office chairs, obviously unable to tell them apart. Todd thought about wiggling his stubby fingers at her, but he doubted she would get the hint.

Todd slumped into an armchair, but its narrow confines couldn't accommodate his bulk. He stood and paced. He'd spent too much time in this office last year with Principal Gray, and he suspected this new principal wouldn't like him either.

His suspicions proved correct two minutes later when Principal Evans emerged from his office. Shit. Principal Gray had been a tired old white man with little energy for disciplining miscreants. This new principal was a tall young Black man with hands large enough to grip a basketball—or a juvenile delinquent's neck—one-handed. His deep-set eyes scanned the surroundings before he added a paper to the secretary's stack.

"Will you enter this information in the student's file, please?" His tone was polite, yet it carried an air of authority that suggested his comment was an order, not a question.

"Of course, sir." The secretary kept her tone polite, but her lips tightened into a thin line.

Principal Evans, either oblivious to her resentment or indifferent, pivoted to return to his office, but he stopped when he caught sight of Todd.

"You have a problem with chairs, son?"

Todd bristled. His own father never called him "son." What made this stranger assume that right?

7

"The chair has a problem with me." Todd didn't bother keeping the sass out of his tone. The teachers would've briefed the new principal on Todd and his brother, so trying to earn the man's good graces was as futile as trying to earn his teammates' forgiveness.

Principal Evans tilted his chin as if sizing him up. "I'll keep that in mind if we ever get funding for new furniture." His tone implied he'd dealt with much tougher kids than Todd, but he disappeared into his office without further comment.

Adam emerged from Mrs. Moore's office and whipped out his phone. "Meet you in the car."

Todd cast one more glance at the principal's door before entering the guidance office and sitting in yet another small seat. He supposed Mrs. Moore liked making her students uncomfortable. A middle-aged white woman with a chickenpox scar above her left eye, Mrs. Moore kept a photo of her teenaged sons on her desk. Both wore private school uniforms. Not proud enough of Brooks High to send your own kids here, eh?

"Well, Todd, I've switched you back into the regular classes. You'll have—"

"I'm not in honors anymore?"

"Principal Gray should never have caved to Coach Harris's whims." The football coach had pushed Todd and Adam into the honors track last year, hoping the higher challenge would keep them out of trouble. He couldn't have been more wrong. "Since you're no longer playing, I see no reason for you to continue."

"I want to stay in honors." Todd couldn't believe the words left his mouth. He'd underperformed in honors last year, but the hope parasite lurched in his stomach, demanding compliance. Claire was in the honors classes.

Mrs. Moore tilted her head. "Adam dropped honors."

"I'm not Adam." Her appeal to his twin's actions only strengthened his resolve. In this one thing, he'd follow his own path. Adam could have any girl he wanted, any girl but Claire.

"Your grades tanked in honors."

"It's senior year. Pad my schedule with electives."

Mrs. Moore tapped her keyboard. "I can get you into honors economics if you take art as an elective." She eyed his left fingers, as if wondering how he'd paint with them.

"Great. Sign me up." Todd stood before she could object. "Anything else?"

Mrs. Moore crossed her arms over her chest, unwilling to cede control. "I'll give you one quarter in honors. If you can't keep your grades up, you drop back to regular. Deal?"

She expected him to fail. Big surprise. Everyone expected him to fail, with good reason. Even when getting into trouble, Adam was the mastermind. Todd was the henchman, good for hitting things and getting high afterward. He'd been a fool to consider seeking her advice about post-high school careers. She didn't even think he'd graduate.

"Deal." *If I'm going to flunk anyway, I may as well flunk in classes with Claire.* Todd strode out of the office with a determined spunk to his stride, but he stopped short as his hope parasite shrank.

Claire hated him.

Chapter 2

Most mothers greeted their seventeen-year-old sons with unwanted questions about their day, but the only reception Todd and Adam received came from the creaking floorboards beneath her bedroom upstairs.

"They're doing it here? Already?" Adam said.

Todd wrinkled his nose. As per their routine, he and Adam trudged to the basement. Neither boy had met their mother's latest conquest, and they didn't care to. She cycled through boyfriends faster than they drank through energy drinks.

Todd donned his headphones, but Adam tapped him on the shoulder before he raised the volume to max. He showed Todd the text.

"Brody says he can get you the 'roids if you're still interested."

"A little late for that." Todd had sought gym juice last year when he'd landed smack in the middle of his wrestling weight class. To stand a chance, he'd either needed to bulk up or drop into a lower class. His devotion to sports didn't surpass his love of cheeseburgers, so he'd opted for the former. Now, it didn't matter. The wrestling team didn't like him any more than the football team did.

"At least you can smoke more," Adam said. His phone chirped, and he grinned as he read the text. "This will cheer you up. Brody says Old Man Caesar agreed to let us set up shop at his place."

Todd perked up. No one knew Caesar's real name or background, only that he was crazy as a cat lady and he grew a special variety of marijuana called the Ides of March. Todd and Adam earned good money selling it in the school's little-monitored old wing. Happy with his cut, the old man was letting them expand their operation.

Todd opened the cracked plastic bin and took inventory of their stash.

"You'd better not smoke that shit in the house," their mother said from the stairway. Her "exercise" had skimmed off her makeup, revealing the oh-so-subtle signs of aging that were devastating for a woman whose primary income derived from indulging rich men's midlife crises.

"Just a quickie, Mom?" Adam said without looking up from his phone. "Did John have to run home to put his kids to bed?"

Todd cringed. Don't taunt her.

Their mother's face twisted. "George is single, and if you want me to keep paying for that phone, you'll find somewhere else to watch porn tomorrow night."

Sure, he's single. That's why he keeps you away from his place.

"Isn't it a mother's job to put a roof over her sons' heads?" Adam said.

"We'd have multiple roofs if not for you."

Todd winced and rubbed the four stumps that used to be his left fingers, but Adam leaped to his feet, towering over their mother.

"That jackass got what he deserved."

Their mother reached into her wallet and handed him a fifty. "Go to the movies or something. I won't wait up."

Adam didn't budge, but Todd snatched the cash. "Have fun, Mom."

He sank back into the couch, dismissing her. Adam lingered, eyes fixed on the staircase long after she disappeared.

"Bitch."

Todd didn't dwell on the ethics of calling your own mother a bitch. It seemed nicer than whore.

"Any ideas for where to retreat tomorrow?"

"Oh, I'm spending the night in Tina Lockard's bed. You can find your own warm bunk."

An image of Claire flashed through Todd's mind, but he banished it. "Nice to know where I rank."

Adam clapped him on the shoulder. "I'll make it up to you."

Todd rolled himself a joint. Adam would fulfill that promise, but Todd wasn't sure he wanted him to.

* * *

After Adam drove off to his date with Tina Lockard, Todd ambled aimlessly around the neighborhood, wishing he could walk to Canada and start a new life.

His subconscious must have had other ideas, because he ended up at school. A sign advertised the volleyball team's first match. Claire. Before he thought better of it, he used his mom's fifty to purchase a ticket and entered the gym.

Whistles, sneaker squeaks, and ball thumps echoed through the space. The stands held a healthy crowd for an early season game. Todd swallowed. None of the fans would appreciate his presence, but returning home was unthinkable. He snuck to the top bleacher and sat by himself. With luck, no one would notice him.

Even from his high perch, Todd picked out Claire and her friends among the uniformed players. The four of them rarely separated. Beth, a beautiful Black girl who was most known for being Jeff Chen's ex-girlfriend, stood by the net. As always, her dour expression warned against any guy attempting to repeat Jeff's betrayal. Next to her stood Maite, who called out something in Spanish. Her inhuman height and martial arts training made her the group's de facto bodyguard. Todd had endured more than one split lip on her account.

At the baseline stood Saafi, a Somali girl who wore a hijab over her hair and leggings and long sleeves beneath her jersey. Todd averted his gaze as guilt assailed him. Last year, Adam had made it his personal mission to see the Muslim girl's hair. Frequent failures made him desperate, and he recruited a group of guys to ambush her—a group that included Todd.

Todd had thought it was no big deal, just hair. Maybe after Adam finally saw it, he'd abandon his obsession with Saafi, and they could go back to smoking, playing video games, and avoiding their mother. But Adam hadn't stopped after ripping off Saafi's hijab.

Maite had rushed to aid her friend, and the situation dissolved into a fist fight. Todd couldn't make himself hit the girls, but he hadn't helped them either. Only Principal Gray's negligence saved him and Adam from greater punishment than a suspension.

That's why Claire hated him. That's why everyone in these stands hated him. *I shouldn't be here.* He stood to leave, but the ref blew the whistle, and teams lined up for the national anthem. No way he could sneak past them. He may as well watch the match.

Claire's red hair fought her braid's confinement, but her green eyes focused on the ball as she prepared to serve. Todd remembered her saying her position rarely served first, but she was the team's most consistent—and powerful—server. True to her word, her serve rocketed over the net, and the other team struggled to receive it.

Todd knew little about volleyball, but Claire's team clearly outmatched their opponents. They played as if connected to a single nervous system. Claire fought hard, her pale face set in grim determination. During their brief period of not-quite-dating, she'd let Todd do all the talking, but on the court, she was as fiery as a stereotypical redhead.

Brooks High won the first set, and the teams switched sides. The next two games finished just as quickly, with Brooks wining in straight sets. The fans cheered, and the girls hugged each other. Todd's chest tightened as he remembered being a part of a team. He shook the feeling away and rubbed his stubby fingers. He had Adam.

Todd leaned against the bleacher behind him, figuring he'd wait until the stands cleared to sneak out last. The crowd thinned, but to his horror, Saafi peeled away from her friends and climbed the bleachers. Todd looked around, but no one else stood nearby. She was heading for him. People called her "Ambassador Saafi" for a reason, but Todd doubted she was coming to make peace with him.

She stopped several feet below him, eyes wary. "Now isn't the time to stalk Claire."

Todd grimaced. He hadn't known what he'd expected, but an accurate assessment of his motivation wasn't it. He tried to play it cool.

"Oh?"

Saafi put her hands on her hips. "You know her dad committed suicide last spring, right?"

The stuffy gym air clogged Todd's suddenly dry throat. Poor Claire. What could he say to her?

As he absorbed the news, Maite, Beth, and Claire noticed their friend's absence and rushed to her, long legs bounding up the bleachers with athletic ease. Soon, three sets of eyes glared at him, and Maite inserted herself between Todd and Saafi.

"Why are you here?" Her accent had improved slightly since last year.

Todd remained seated, hoping they wouldn't see him as a threat. "I..." I wanted to see Claire? I wanted to escape my mother's new boyfriend? They wouldn't accept either rationale.

"Sssssstay away from Saafi." Claire's stutter elongated the first s. She nodded to her friends, and they herded Saafi down the bleachers.

"Claire, wait." Todd scrambled to his feet and grabbed her arm, but she yanked it free.

"And stay away from me."

Todd's hope parasite withered as she departed, just like his new marigold plant would. She thinks I'm a monster.

She was right.

CHAPTER 3

Todd tensed as his tennis shoe squeaked on the locker room floor, but the football team was still outside practicing.

"Adam, are you sure about this?"

Adam gave him a patronizing look. "If we don't return fire, they'll think they won."

Who cares? They wouldn't see any of their former teammates after graduation anyway. What did it matter if they won a petty squabble?

"Scared, Todd?" Big Brody said. The ruddy-skinned oaf used to be called Cupcake Brody on account of his fondness for pastries, but his last growth spurt killed the nickname. No one dared tease him now.

Todd addressed Adam, refusing to acknowledge the dig. "This better not be your idea of repaying me for leaving you the car so you could sleep at Tina's."

"This is revenge," Adam said, sneaking farther into the locker room. "Making it up to you will involve girls. I even promise they'll be pretty." He grinned. "What did you end up doing, anyway?"

"Nothing."

Big Brody snorted. "He got shot down by Jeff's ex."

"What? No!" Todd said.

"Multiple people saw you at the volleyball game, man."

"Not Jeff's ex," Adam said. "You still have a thing for the redhead, don't you?" He grimaced. "Dude, why?"

"C-c-claire?" Big Brody chuckled. "God, can you imagine what she's like in bed?" He raised his pitch in a poor imitation of a feminine voice. "Oh, T-t-t-todd. You sssssssexy b-b-beast!"

15

"Shut up," Todd snapped. Claire's stutter was number one hundred on the list of ways to describe her. Why did everyone jump to that first? "Are we doing this or not?"

"Yeah, yeah. Simmer down, bro." Adam gestured to Big Brody, who pulled several bottles of shaving cream out of his backpack. They emptied them into the football players' shoes and gym bags, and Adam wrote nasty messages on the mirror and on Cumar's locker.

They piled the empty bottles near Jeff Chen's locker and hurried out, only to bump into a human wall—Principal Evans.

"Todd. Adam. Brody," he said, pointing at each boy.

Shit. He hadn't even glanced at Todd's fingers to tell them apart.

"I don't recall seeing your names on the team roster," the principal said dryly. "I suppose you're making mischief?"

Todd's insides shook, but Adam shrugged. "You can't give us detention before school has even started."

Principal Evans smiled. "No, but I can charge you for damages to school property. Shaving cream can discolor the paint." He gestured to a blob that had clung to Big Brody's arm hair. "You can pay the fine or work it off with the custodian. Your choice."

"Pay it," Adam said, likely already thinking of a loophole.

"I'll expect the money in my office by the first day of school." Principal Evans strolled away without another word, businesslike in his attitude. Todd didn't know what to make of him, but Adam curled his lip.

"Fool." Adam pulled a cigarette from his pocket and stormed out the door. Todd moved to follow, but a pair of voices caught his ear. He peered around the corner and spotted the volleyball team on a water break from practice. The voices belonged to the Gossip Girls, who, despite not being related, dressed identically and always had their heads together, blonde ponytails wagging as they related the latest school scandals.

"...I hear his fingers got eaten by a rabid dog, and if you look closely, you can still see the teeth marks."

Todd rubbed his four stubs. He didn't have a right to feel hurt after pranking his former teammates, but the words still cut into him.

"Hey," Claire snapped. "Cut it out."

"Geez, Claire, I didn't know you still had a thing for him."

"I have nothing for him. I'm against making ffffun of people for things they c-can't control."

Claire must command a good amount of respect from her teammates, because they shut up and moved away. She drank from the fountain, but Beth, Maite, and Saafi surrounded her.

"Claire?" Beth asked. "You don't still have a thing for him, do you?"

"I'd rather kiss my garbage disposal," Claire said. Her voice quieted. "Just...not because of his fingers."

The world tilted as Todd lost his equilibrium. Even though Claire hated him, she still defended him. He didn't know how to interpret her defense, but it warmed him nonetheless.

The far doors opened, and the football team strode through. Todd shook off his good feeling and sprinted out the front entrance before the players caught sight of him.

"What kept you?" Adam said, crushing his cigarette butt on the ground beside their car.

"Just drive," Todd said.

Adam shrugged, and they drove to one of their favorite smoke spots. Todd relaxed on the wooden park bench. His teammates would know he and Adam pulled that prank, but at least Todd wouldn't have to see their reactions. Seeing Saafi at the game had affected him more than he'd expected. Hurting people was easier when you didn't witness their pain.

Adam whistled at a pair of girls jogging in their sports bras. Usually Todd would admire them as well, but he couldn't help thinking neither girl would have defended him as Claire had. As if to confirm his suspicion, the girls gave Adam the finger, but he just laughed. He puffed on the joint once more before crushing the stub into the pavement.

"Hey, let's get some sundaes," Adam said.

"From Cream Peaks? When did we last eat there?" The ice cream parlor was famous for serving sundaes with scoops the size of softballs.

Adam grinned. "Afraid you'll lose to me in your old age?"

"Fat chance. I'm the one who's still working out every day." They trotted to the shop. The kids in line wrinkled their noses and shifted away from them, but the workers didn't comment as they scooped two massive sundaes.

As per their tradition, Todd and Adam raced to see who could finish the treat first. Todd won.

"Lucky break," Adam said.

"Yeah right. You still have half a scoop left." Todd yanked his brother's sundae out of his hands and polished it off.

Adam laughed. "Guess all that gardening gives you an appetite."

Todd grinned, stomach satisfied for now. Adam joked about their eating contests, but his losing was a noble habit. When they were little, their mother hadn't always filled their fridge. Mrs. Thompson would feed them, and Adam would sneak Todd extra food whenever he could, even if it meant he went hungry. They shopped for themselves now, but Todd would never forget those childhood sacrifices.

Good thing they'd stuffed themselves, because their mother met them with an ambush instead of a home-cooked meal. Her eyes, ringed with too much eyeliner, resembled a shotgun muzzle.

"Your principal called. Says we owe the school three hundred dollars for paint?"

Uh-oh. Usually their mother stayed out of their lives, but money always attracted her attention.

"He called me during a date," she continued. "You stupid little shits. Can't you stay out of trouble for five minutes?" She swung her purse, hitting Todd in the shoulder.

"Relax, Mom," Adam said, but his face paled a little. Principal Gray wouldn't have bothered to phone parents. He wouldn't have bothered disciplining them at all for such a small prank. "We'll take care of it."

"With your own money. Get a job, sell your phone, I don't care, but I'm not paying for this." She grabbed her purse from where it had fallen to the floor. "Now, if you'll excuse me, I have a date to apologize to." She stormed out, high heels clacking.

The ice cream in Todd's stomach churned. This new principal may talk calmly, but he obviously didn't put up with any crap.

"How are we going to handle this?"

"By paying a visit to Old Man Caesar," Adam replied with a grin.

* * *

Old Man Caesar's setup was far less sophisticated than Mrs. Thompson and Noah's garden center, but Todd had made some improvements over the last couple of years. He weeded, fertilized, and watered the plants well. Under his care, the Ides of March thrived, much to the old man's delight.

Todd yanked a couple weeds as Adam negotiated.

"If you let us use your shed to store the stuff, we'll give you a cut."

"I don't know." The scrawny, pale man pawed his scraggly gray beard. "This is getting too complicated for me."

Adam and Todd had stumbled upon the old man a couple of years ago while avoiding one of their mother's boyfriends. He grew for his own recreation, but Adam convinced him to let them sell his stuff. Now Adam wanted to use the old man's shed as his base of operations.

"We'll handle the complicated. You just give us a key and accept the money." Adam gave the old man the smile he used to get girls' numbers.

"You sure I'll have enough for me?"

"Absolutely." Adam gestured to Todd. "He may be missing fingers, but he has two green thumbs."

With that, they spat and shook hands, Caesar's deal-sealing ritual. The old man truly was batty, perhaps from years of smoking more than he ate or drank. Would Todd become a crazy old man if he maintained his habits? Maybe he should cut back, focus more on selling the Ides of March than smoking it. Better yet, he could focus on growing the marijuana and let Adam handle sales. He doubted pot grower was on Mrs. Moore's list of post-high school career tracks, but who cared? Any job that earned him enough money to leave his mom's house sounded good to him.

Todd paused his weeding to stretch. While the old man's yard wasn't the garden center, he couldn't argue with the location. Caesar's dilapidated house was one of two on a gravel cul-de-sac surrounded by enough woods to allow him to pretend they were in the country instead of near downtown Minneapolis. The remnants of a third house lay burned to ashes. Todd had always wondered what happened to it.

Todd finished his stretching, but a movement in the second house caught his eye. A pale girl peered at him from the second-story window. She caught him looking and disappeared behind a curtain, but her image stuck with Todd, as if she were a ghost warning him of trouble to come.

"It's all set," Adam said. Todd jumped as his brother thumped him on the shoulder. "Our financial woes are over. I bet Principal Moron flips when we hand him the cash."

"Great." Todd's words emerged halfhearted as he wondered whether this latest development in their "summer job" was what the girl was warning him about.

CHAPTER 4

For the first time in Todd's memory, he and Adam arrived early to school. Other early birds flocked together to chat, but the twins no longer had friends to update on their summer antics. They had each other, of course, but Todd and his brother weren't starting this year any better than they'd ended last year.

Principal Evans accepted their cash envelope as calmly as he might retrieve a dropped pencil. Todd waited for something—a scowl, a harsh word, anything—but the principal merely said, "Anything else?"

Todd breathed out in relief as they left the office, but Adam seethed. "Who does he think he is, anyway?"

"Does it matter? We're off the hook."

Adam halted. "Respect matters, Todd. You can't let people walk all over you." He gripped Todd's left shoulder, but Todd felt the reminder in his stubby fingers. Todd wouldn't label Principal Evans's failure to acknowledge Adam's criminal genius as disrespectful, but Adam had always navigated the social universe with greater mastery than Todd.

"Whatever." Todd shook free of Adam's grip as the bell rang, summoning students to their first classes. He considered sneaking to the old wing for a pre-class smoke, but he didn't think it wise to risk the principal's ire so soon after their last encounter. Besides, his first class was his easy A—art.

His decision to forego smoking proved wise, as the art room lay beyond what felt like miles of twisting corridors and down a half-flight of stairs. He held his breath as he entered the room, not sure what to expect. A mix of grade levels sat at broad black-topped tables spread about a room so spacious, Todd wondered why it hadn't been commandeered for other purposes. Perhaps whoever was in charge had forgotten about this room. It housed every imaginable piece of art equipment, but it showed more signs of neglect than Old Man Caesar's shack.

A kiln squatted in the far corner. Paint sets lined the wall in the haphazard fashion of kindergarteners lining up for lunch. A row of blank canvases leaned against each other like dominoes too tired to push their companions over. Pastels, charcoal, and crayons were piled unceremoniously in separate bins. Other items Todd wouldn't have associated with art—plastic bottles, rubber bands, an old pair of shoes—were heaped in a wooden barrel labeled THE POOL OF INSPIRATION.

Todd recognized the Gossip Girls sitting in the front right, blonde ponytails bobbing as they whispered to each other. Though his reputation couldn't get worse, he figured he ought to avoid them. He traversed the dusty floor toward the back left, where an Asian girl he didn't recognize had pulled her wheelchair up to the table. She crossed her arms over her chest as he sat beside her.

"I know who you are." Accusation laced her tone.

Great, even people I've never met hate me. Todd busied himself digging for nothing in his backpack.

When he didn't respond, she continued. "I'm Beth Jones's sister."

He examined her, trying to work out the genetics behind a Black girl with an Asian sister. She let him bumble for a moment before saying, "I'm adopted, stupid."

"Oh." Todd didn't know what else to say, but the girl plopped her backpack onto the one remaining seat at the table.

"I'm saving this for a friend, so your other half will have to sit elsewhere."

"He's not in this class," Todd said.

She raised an exceptionally articulate eyebrow.

Todd scowled. "We're not conjoined."

She looked about to respond, but another girl rushed toward them. Todd froze, thinking he'd seen a ghost. Her face, pale as a blank page, was pinched, and her eyes—which hovered somewhere between hazel, green, and gray—filled with worry. There was no mistaking the mysterious girl who'd spied him at Old Man Caesar's.

She set her tattered backpack on the table beside the first girl. "Am I late?"

"I told you art was in Timbuktu," the first girl said.

A half-smile flashed across the blonde girl's face. "Did you know Timbuktu is a real place? It's a city in northern Mali that was founded in the twelfth century and later became extraordinarily wealthy. Most European explorations failed, however, hence its use to denote someplace so far away as to be impossible to reach."

"Cat, it is way too early in the morning for me to discuss etymologies with human encyclopedias."

The second girl chuckled and moved to sit down, but she flinched when she noticed Todd.

She flinched. Todd had never been as smooth as Adam, but girls usually didn't fear him. He tried a poor imitation of Adam's disarming grin.

"I'm Todd."

"I know who you are," the girl whispered. She fidgeted with her ponytail and scooted closer to her friend's wheelchair. "I'm Cathryn Banks."

"And I'm Minh Don't-Mess-with-My-Friend Jones," the other girl said.

Before he could answer, the teacher strolled into the room. His short stature meant his baggy shorts reached below his knees, and the rest of his hairy, muscular legs poked out beneath him. His pale, bald head sported a tattoo of a laughing cartoon rabbit. Instead of striding to the blackboard, he jumped on top of his desk and raised his bulky arms into the air.

"Today, we begin our journey into the arts. I'm Mr. Martin, but my fellow artistes"—he gestured to the class—"may call me Oliver. For our first lesson, explore the various tools of creation around the room. Take paints, pastels, pencils...anything you like, and do anything you want with them. Our goal is to explore their essence like innocent children." He broadened his arms as though hugging the room, and Todd reconsidered his smoking habits. Forget Old Man Caesar; this must be the long-term effects of pot use. Judging by Cathryn's expression, she was reconsidering something too.

"I should have stayed in choir."

"Relax, Cat," Minh said. "He's a kook, but he won't damage your perfect GPA. I'll help you. Besides, we're finally in a class together." Cathryn opened her mouth to object, but Minh cut her off. "Come on, I need to use the bathroom."

"Why do girls always pee in packs?" The question tumbled out of Todd's mouth of its own accord. He'd always wondered, but never asked. Perhaps because he wasn't angling for a date with the younger girls—sophomores by his guess—his subconscious had found them less intimidating.

Minh's glare taught his subconscious otherwise. "I wouldn't leave my dog alone with you, much less my friend." She wheeled away with a cocky toss of her inky black hair. Cathryn followed, ironically resembling an obedient puppy.

Todd retrieved a piece of charcoal, but he didn't know how to use it. Explore its essence? What did that even mean? He hoped Minh had spoken the truth about the kook of a teacher not hurting their GPAs.

He rubbed the black stick between his fingers, smudging them. His mood darkened. Though he was used to soil sticking beneath his fingernails, the charcoal stain seemed more ominous, as if representing last year's unforgivable sins.

"She doesn't have a dog." Cathryn appeared a table and a half away. Her eyes flitted to the door, but she'd directed her comment at Todd.

"What?"

"Minh. She doesn't have a dog. I just...I figured you'd want to know."

"Right, thanks." He didn't know how to transition into his next question, but this might be his only chance to catch her without her tough friend. "Could you not tell anyone you saw me at Old Man Caesar's?"

She wrinkled her forehead. "Anyone could tell you smoke, Todd."

"Huh?"

"You smell." She stepped backward as if afraid her insult would trigger something. Todd kept his seat, even though her honesty made him cringe. He couldn't afford to scare her off. The Ides of March was making

Todd and Adam good money. If word got out about their source, they'd lose their monopoly and have to ask their mother for gas money.

"Okay, true, but I'd still like to keep my...after-school project to myself."

Cathryn wove her skinny fingers into the end of her ponytail. "I don't care what you do with my neighbor's marijuana, but stay away from my house, okay?"

"Deal." Todd gave her a warm smile, but she fled the room, no doubt rejoining her friend in whatever girls-only rituals took place in the bathroom. When the pair returned, Cathryn behaved as if their conversation never happened. She picked up a colored pencil and wrote something.

"Think beyond typical use," Oliver said, peering at her paper. Though he stood next to where she sat, his head rose only about six inches taller than hers. "Like your friend." He gestured to where Minh was doodling with her own art pens. Todd blinked. How had she drawn that so quickly? Her ink-stained fingers were already adding the finishing touches to a fire-breathing variation of the teacher's scalp tattoo.

Mr. Martin—Oliver, Todd reminded himself—skipped to the next table like a little girl playing hopscotch. Todd exchanged a glance with Cathryn as the bell signaled the end of the period, glad he wasn't the only one who'd be completely lost in this class.

He checked his schedule as the room emptied. Next came honors economics—on the opposite side of the building. He raced up the half-flight of stairs and charged through the hallways, glad his summer of greenhouse labor had kept him in even better shape than football. Even so, the bell rang just before he crossed the classroom threshold.

"Look who it is," Beth Jones said from the front row. Her eyebrows weren't as articulate as her adopted sister's, but she held herself with a similar defensive posture. Guess genetics isn't everything.

Saafi sat beside her, notebooks organized atop her desk and one of those ten ton mom-purses tucked underneath it. As the future valedictorian, she'd have nothing to fear in an honors class, but she shifted her position as Todd passed. Claire, who sat behind Saafi, didn't even spare Todd a glance. Until he sat next to her. Then her green eyes flashed.

"D-don't you want to save a seat for Adam?" She gestured to the back row, where two seats sat empty.

"We're not conjoined," Todd said for the second time, wishing he'd tried harder to keep the annoyance from his tone.

The teacher began class before Claire could respond. He introduced himself as Mr. Patel, emphasis on the Mr., and stood erect behind the podium, the exact opposite of the art teacher. Where Oliver was short, stocky, pale, and hairy everywhere but his head, Mr. Patel was tall, slender, amber-skinned, and hairless apart from a head of thick black hair, which he wore in a fashionable cut that matched his classy attire. Todd guessed they wouldn't be "exploring the essence" of economics in this class.

"Now that you know me, I'd like each of you to introduce yourself as if you were a businessman or woman meeting with potential investors."

Todd had no clue what that meant, but Saafi demonstrated it perfectly. She rose to her feet gracefully.

"I'm Saafi Khalif, and I'm delighted to make your acquaintance. I'm sure we'll have an excellent semester." She returned to her seat, earning herself an approving nod from Mr. Patel.

Claire stood next, meeting the teacher's eye with a defiant glare. "I'm Claire P-peterson. I sssss-ssssstutter, but you'll get used to it." She dropped into her seat without looking for a response from her teacher.

Attagirl, Claire. When they'd first met, she'd shied away from speaking in class, but something changed last year. Though her speech had improved—she'd given entire speeches without stuttering—she put the onus on her teachers to learn to listen instead of constantly exhausting herself to avoid stuttering. Todd couldn't help admiring her spunk.

Mr. Patel must have thought otherwise, because he frowned before gesturing to the student behind Claire to introduce himself. After the class introductions finished, he led them through the usual drivel about behavioral expectations.

Todd's mind drifted, and he snuck glances at Claire. Given the choice between the identical twins, girls always chose Adam. Whether they did so because Adam was more charismatic or because he had all his fingers, Todd didn't know. Claire had been the first to choose him, and though she lacked other girls' looks, her selectivity alone attracted Todd.

At first, she'd smiled and nodded through conversations and passively accepted his advances, but after the incident with Saafi, she transformed. She stood as firm as an ancient redwood and fought with more intensity than a lightning storm. She'd told Todd she never wanted to see him again, but her backbone only made her more attractive. He hadn't known what he'd had until he lost it.

When Mr. Patel reached the end of the syllabus, he raised his voice, as if ensuring anyone who'd drifted off started paying attention again.

"A significant portion of your grade will derive from a year-long partner project in which you will develop a business. We'll start with market research next week, but for tomorrow, begin brainstorming ideas. Your partner is whomever is sitting to next to you." He gestured down the columns, and Todd's hope parasite did a back flip. He sat beside Claire, and Mr. Patel had paired them together.

Claire's hand shot up. "C-can't we work in a group of three?" She gestured to Beth and Saafi, probably wishing Maite were in the honors courses instead of Todd.

"No."

"But—"

"No buts. I am the teacher, which means I am in charge." A grin plucked the corners of his mouth. "Don't worry. You'll get used to it."

Claire glowered at Todd, but her anger did nothing to quash his good feeling. He thought of the marigold plant in his room, which was still alive despite several days in his care. Maybe that was a sign. This was his chance to win her back.

He just had to keep Adam away from her.

CHAPTER 5

F ifi's claws clattered behind Todd as he hefted the hose to the register. "You can't start your own greenhouse," Noah said as he added the fall clearance discount. "Then you won't help here anymore."

Todd offered him a reassuring grin. "You won't get rid of me that easily."

If anything, Todd's involvement with Old Man Caesar's marijuana plot necessitated more time in the garden center. Noah wasn't much of a teacher, so Todd had needed to pay close attention to learn the plant whisperer's secrets.

Todd offered Fifi a scratch before hauling his hose to the car and driving to the derelict cul-de-sac. Shadows fell over Caesar's house, a sign of the shortening days. Adam was talking with Big Brody and a couple other guys Todd didn't recognize. He didn't bother greeting them before reaching the spigot and removing the old hose. He hated that thing. It was thin, kinked easily, and always tangled no matter how carefully he coiled it. Perhaps Noah had spoiled him, but Todd decreed Old Man Caesar was due for an upgrade.

"What are you doing?" The old man's eyes flitted between Todd and Adam's group, clearly uncomfortable about relinquishing control.

"Relax, I paid for it." Todd fitted the new hose to the spigot and set up the reel, which would allow him to coil it neatly after he finished watering the plants. Without another word to Caesar or Adam, he strolled between the rows. Sometimes, Todd preferred leaves and stems to flesh and blood.

He glanced at the other house's second-story window, but he didn't see Cathryn. He finished watering a row, and she burst through the trees across the street. She raced toward her house, but tripped near the dumpster, dropping something. Gravel rumbled down the road, announcing a car's arrival. Her already pale face blanched, and she rushed to her front door without picking up whatever she'd dropped.

Someone is late for dinner. Moments later, an old gray sedan parked in front of Cathryn's house, and a large man with dark hair and skin a shade less pale than Cathryn's emerged. He grumbled as he unlocked the door—Cathryn must have relocked it—and entered the house.

Todd finished watering, pleased with his new hose. He reeled it in, but Adam was still chatting with the guys. Feeling unsociable, Todd jogged to the dumpster to investigate Cathryn's fallen item.

He picked up a hardcover book and brushed the dirt off the spine. Word by Word: The Secret Life of Dictionaries. Cathryn had interesting tastes. Todd tucked the book under his arm and ambled to the front door, but he hesitated. Cathryn had asked him to stay away from her house, but she'd want her book back, right?

"Hey, Todd," Adam called. "Come here."

Todd glanced at the door, but if Cathryn's dad was that strict about being home by dinnertime, he wouldn't want a pot smoker showing up on her porch. I'll give her the book in art on Monday.

Satisfied with his decision, Todd joined the guys.

Adam grinned. "Told you I'd make it up to you. Jeremy here invited us to his cousin's party." He smacked the shoulder of the guy standing next to him.

"I need to shower first." Todd gestured to his soiled clothes.

Adam wrinkled his nose. "Yeah, you do." He turned to the others. "We'll see you there."

He took the keys from Todd and drove them home. Their mother would be absent all weekend. With more notice, they could have thrown a party of their own. More notice, and the ping-pong table they'd asked Santa for until they realized his face changed every year and he only brought presents for their mom.

Todd ran the shower extra hot, letting the heat soak into his stiff muscles as the water blasted the sweat and dirt off his body. The relaxation made an early bedtime appealing.

He wandered into their shared room, and Adam threw a shirt at him. Ugh. The party.

"Cheer up, man. You look like someone died," Adam said.

Todd checked his marigold. "Nope. Still alive."

Adam chuckled. "You've been spending too much time in the greenhouse. Time for some nightlife."

"I don't know. I'm wiped." Todd looked longingly at his bed as he pulled on his jeans and shirt.

"Come on. It'll be good for you." Adam grinned.

Todd glanced over his brother's shoulder. "What's that?" He pointed to a piece of paper taped to the wall near Adam's bed. Closer examination revealed it was the picture of their father with his wife and kids, but Adam had added googly eyes and alien antennas.

"Want it for your art class?"

Todd shook his head. He doubted turning his half-siblings into Martians equated "finding their essence."

"Man, you are in the pits today." Adam stared at him. "It's the redhead, isn't it?"

"What? No." *Is it so hard to believe I'm just tired and want to sleep?*

Adam rolled his eyes. "You need this party. Forget Claire. I'll find you a prettier girl, one who can talk."

Claire can talk. She spoke better than Noah, but Todd didn't point that out. Acquiescing to Adam's badgering would be easier than fighting it. Besides, he might enjoy partying with people who didn't know about last year.

"All right." Todd finished dressing, and Adam drove them across town. Of course the festivities were across town. No one nearby invited them to parties anymore.

Loud music blared in Todd's ears, making him wish for the quiet plants. *Adam is right. I'm becoming a hermit.* He forced a smile as he followed Adam to the back porch, grabbing a beer along the way. Todd looked around for someone with a cigarette, but no one smoked. He wished he'd brought some Ides of March. Without it, he'd need stronger alcohol than beer to get in a festive mood.

Adam didn't need chemical help to socialize. He charged into the fray and made himself the center of attention by relating one of his previous pranks. Todd leaned against the railing, nursing his beer. It smelled like Fifi's wet fur and tasted just as bad. He drank it anyway, downing it quickly so he had an excuse to grab another drink.

A lanky guy stumbled in front of the porch door. Todd weaved around him and hopped over another guy who'd fallen on the kitchen floor. He scooped himself a glass of what he hoped was strong punch, and when he returned to the porch, Adam was waiting for him, a girl on each arm.

"See, ladies. I told you I'm a clone."

A girl with jet black hair, tanned skin, and boobs that threatened to break out of her shirt separated from Adam and approached Todd.

"Did you really lose your fingers fighting off a police dog?"

Todd shot Adam a glare before lying. "Something like that."

If Adam noticed the glare, he didn't react. He tugged the remaining girl away, hands already creeping to her backside.

"Wow," the dark-haired girl said. She reached for him, but tripped over her heels. Todd caught her, and she giggled. "Thanks."

Todd righted her, and she gave him a glassy-eyed stare. He thought of the moment he'd met Claire. She'd dropped her purse in a crowd, and its contents had scattered. After he'd helped her up, she'd looked at him as if he'd lifted a boulder over his head instead of handing her lip balm. He hadn't needed to lie about his fingers to earn her admiration. A random act of kindness had done it.

"Can you take me somewhere less...outside?" The girl wobbled. Evidently, she'd drunk a lot more punch than Todd had.

"Uh, sure." Todd stabilized the stumbling girl with an arm around her waist and guided her inside.

"I waaaant another," the girl said.

I don't think you do. Before Todd could say anything, she grabbed someone else's punch. In her sloppy attempt to drink it, she dumped half of it down her shirt. As the pink stain spread over her breasts, her face contorted like a toddler having a tantrum.

"I liked this shirt."

A burly guy bumped her from behind, and she toppled to the floor and burst into tears. Todd glanced around. No one paid her any attention. Was he responsible for this chick just because Adam set them up? Probably. Adam usually arranged for them to date a pair of friends, and girls talked. If he left her on the floor, she'd bad-talk him to all her friends, and then he and Adam wouldn't find dates at their school ever again. Since they couldn't find dates at their own school anymore, they couldn't afford to be blacklisted.

The girl's sobs stopped almost as quickly as they began. She laid her head on someone's shoe and closed her eyes. Todd lifted her into his arms, intending to find her a safer place to sleep off the alcohol, but she opened her eyes, ogling him as if he were a swimsuit model.

"You're strong."

Todd carried her past a group of card players, but when they reached a less crowded hallway, the girl flipped out of his hands. She tugged his shirt and pursed her lips.

With a clear invitation like that, Todd should've already had his tongue down her throat and his hands down her shorts, but his mouth tasted like ashes. This girl, whose name he still didn't know, was...boring. Needy and boring. He could sleep with her with zero repercussions, but did he want that? He'd always lived in the moment, but his conversation with the guidance counselor got him thinking long term. Did he want to live like a high school party guy forever, cycling through partners like his mom?

Not getting the response she wanted, the girl pressed herself against him, and his body decided to hell with philosophical speculation. Nothing mattered more than getting inside her pants. She kissed him, missing his mouth and catching his chin. He moved to kiss her properly, but he caught a whiff of her perfume. It was the same one his mother used.

Todd pushed her away so fast she fell to the ground again. "I'm sorry."

Forgetting any sense of responsibility for his arranged date, he shoved through the crowds and burst through the front door. He gulped the chill autumn air, dying for a cigarette.

What's wrong with me? What sort of idiot turned down easy sex with a beautiful girl? He'd never had this problem. Then he met Claire. No, then he'd lost Claire.

When they'd been semi-dating, she'd been just another girl, albeit more fun than that needy chick. Claire had approached partying with the same intensity as sports—full throttle, no brakes. If you couldn't keep up, she'd leave you behind. Then she changed. Big muscles and alleged fights with police dogs wouldn't impress her, not anymore. Todd wasn't sure what produced the shift, but her newfound confidence suggested she'd found something better than partying. He couldn't help wanting to be someone she found attractive, even if he wasn't sure how.

Stupid. Stupid. Stupid. He smacked himself, hoping to pound some sense into his head. Adam would brand this incident onto Todd's forehead if he discovered the truth. To save his reputation, he should find another girl to sleep with—one who didn't remind him of his mother's neediness—but he couldn't make himself move. He wished he'd stayed home.

Todd sat on the steps and thought up a convincing lie to tell Adam. Until his brother finished partying, Todd was stranded.

CHAPTER 6

Oliver—Todd decided he couldn't bring himself to think of the ridiculous art teacher as "Mr. Martin"—didn't even acknowledge Todd's late arrival. The class was already full, apart from a table where Cathryn sat by herself.

"Where's your friend?" Todd asked as he set his backpack across from her.

"Dentist." Cathryn spoke so quietly, Todd had to strain to hear her. She gestured to her paper. "We're supposed to draw how we felt last night on one side, and how we felt when we woke up on the other." She'd drawn a simple smiley face on both sides.

"They pay him to come up with this stuff?" Todd said as he rummaged through his backpack. He pulled out the book and slid it to Cathryn. "You dropped this the other day."

Cathryn eyed him warily, but her fingers twitched, and after a moment's hesitation, she snatched the book and clutched it to her chest. Had she not looked so serious when she'd done it, Todd would have laughed.

"Thank you," she whispered. She scooted an inch farther away and cracked open the book, but she kept stealing glances at Todd, as if wishing he would leave. With her more dominant friend absent, Todd would've thought Cathryn would speak more freely, but the opposite was true. It was as if Minh were her social battery, and without her, Cathryn retreated into herself.

"Just trying to do a good deed."

She evaluated his statement before speaking. "'It takes many good deeds to build a good reputation, and only one bad one to lose it.' Benjamin Franklin."

"Is that your way of saying you don't trust me?"

"'Love all, trust a few, do wrong to none.' Shakespeare."

"Do you always speak in quotes?"

Cathryn's cheeks reddened. "I like history." She buried her nose in her book, closing the conversation. Todd could hear Adam's voice in his head, demanding he intimidate her so she wouldn't report them, but he'd rather earn her trust. Drawing out her quirky side had been a good start, but she'd scooted farther away and held the book like a shield.

Focus on art. Todd contemplated his blank paper and considered the day's assignment. How had he felt last night? Exhausted. One day's rest after that party hadn't been enough. After catching his breath, he'd gone back inside and found the girl passed out in the hallway. He'd carried her to an empty room and set her where he hoped she could sleep off her intoxication in peace. Adam had appeared just as he emerged. They'd exchanged knowing grins and driven home without talking, but even the nonverbal lie cost Todd a piece of his sanity.

Oliver's voice boomed from behind him, praising a student's "moving visual commentary about the emotional transitional phase of sleep." Todd scribbled a squiggly line and added a straight line to the opposite side of the page, finishing just as the teacher arrived.

"What do you have here?"

"Uh." Todd turned to the straight line. "It's a straight line for when you're asleep, because you're lying down." He flipped the page. "This is for when you're awake, because your brain is thinking and stuff."

Oliver tapped his chin. "Exploring the relative peace of sleep compared with the twisted chaos of waking life. Brilliant." He clapped Todd on the shoulder, but he frowned at Cathryn's drawing. "I think you interpreted the prompt a little too literally."

"It's a happy face, because last night I was reading a book." She flipped the page over. "And another happy face, because now I'm reading another book." She held up the volume as if the key to happiness lay within its pages.

"Well, it's a start, but try to think beyond conventional symbols. Like Todd."

As soon as the teacher turned his back on them, Cathryn shot him a glare. Todd tried to restrain his chuckle, but it still emerged as a snort. The bell rang, and he zipped out of class.

No matter how fast he moved, passing time never lasted long enough for him to arrive at economics before the next bell rang. Mr. Patel pressed his lips into a thin line and gestured for Todd to take his seat beside Claire.

"We're brainstorming ideas for the project," she said. "I d-don't suppose you've come up with any?"

Shit. Between the greenhouse, the marijuana plot, and the party, Todd hadn't even thought about school.

Claire opened her notebook, as if she'd been expecting that. "We're opening a restaurant. Sit-down, fusion cuisine, mmmmoderate pricing. I haven't nailed down a lllllocation yet."

"Wow, you've put a lot of thought into this already."

Claire shrugged. "I want to open my-my-my own restaurant someday, so I may as well start now."

"You like to cook?" Why didn't he know that?

Her green eyes flashed. "No, I like giving people food poisoning."

"Sorry, dumb question." Maybe he was too stupid for honors classes. "I think it's cool that you want to be a chef."

"Really?"

"Yeah, I mean, cooking is useful. The best I can do is put a frozen pizza in the oven."

Claire smiled. A genuine smile. Claire wasn't attractive by most guys' standards—muscular limbs, small boobs, wild hair, and skin that freckled instead of tanned—but she had a great smile and a cute bunny-like nose that wiggled when she laughed. Seeing that smile, Todd's hope parasite wrapped around his heart and squeezed so hard he thought he might pass out. Then she remembered she hated him and scowled, and his heart returned to a trudging pace.

"We should research the market to find a good location." She continued talking, but Todd fixated on a stray hair that had fallen out of her braid. He had a sudden urge to brush it away from her face. This weekend, he could've slept with a much prettier girl, but in that moment, he wanted nothing more than to tuck that strand behind Claire's ear. A simple motion, but somehow it felt a thousand times more intimate than sex with a drunk.

His body temperature skyrocketed as he pictured his fingers tracing her cream-colored skin. Would she flinch if he used his left hand? No. She was anything but squeamish, and she'd showed multiple times that his stubby fingers didn't freak her out. He wouldn't have to make up some heroic story about how he'd lost the tips with her.

"Todd?"

Todd blinked back to reality. "Sounds like a great idea."

"You weren't even listening." Claire packed up her notebooks.

"No, I—"

"If you won't t-t-take this seriously, why should I take you seriously?"

The bell rang before Todd could respond, and Claire left with Beth and Saafi. Her words dripped into his heart, a slow poison for his hope parasite.

Why should she take him seriously?

* * *

Todd finally figured out a strategy for arriving on time to art. He asked Adam to drop him off near a little-used side entrance. He had to jimmy the lock, which froze his fingers in the chilly mornings, but the effort proved worthwhile. Today he'd arrived before the teacher. *Now if I can teleport to economics, I'll be set.*

He sat in what was becoming his usual seat—near the back with the sophomore girls. Though Minh had a sharp tongue, she tolerated him well enough that he didn't deem moving worthwhile. Still, he was enjoying the quiet before she arrived.

He pulled out a piece of scratch paper, determined to list the reasons Claire should get back together with him, but his rationale so far was pitiful. What could he offer her? Claire had a life plan already. Todd's plans included smoking weed and avoiding his mother. Claire aced her classes and her volleyball serves. Todd didn't belong in the honors track and fizzled out of sports. Claire spoke out against bullies, even though she stuttered. Todd teetered on the line between "prankster" and "criminal."

The more he considered the matter, the more he admired Claire—and disapproved of himself. Maybe Mrs. Moore was right. He'd never amount to anything, much less someone worth dating.

The other students filtered in, but Oliver hadn't showed his face. Was it wrong to hope for a more sensible substitute, or better yet, a free period to think?

Minh wheeled to her usual place next to him, towing Cathryn behind her by the invisible bonds of friendship.

"How are your teeth?" Todd asked.

Minh's grin had a knife's edge. "Sparkling perfection, just like the rest of me."

Todd snorted. He didn't know Beth Jones well, but he pitied her. Minh couldn't be an easy little sister.

"What are you working on?" Cathryn slipped into the seat across from him.

Todd tried to cover his paper, but Minh snatched it.

"'My Admirable Qualities,'" she read. Apparently, his list warranted a double eyebrow raise. "The only thing listed is 'nice hair.'"

Cathryn squinted at him. "Is that a popular style among guys?"

"Cat, we need to get you out of the library more often," Minh said. "But to answer your question, Todd's hair won't win him any dates."

"My hair is lush and manly," Todd said, realizing too late how unmanly that sounded. This was why Adam talked to girls, not him. "If girls aren't attracted to great hair, what is attractive?"

"Have you tried being a decent human being?" Minh's words sliced sharper than scissors.

Before Todd processed that statement, Oliver arrived, carrying a recycling container that was bigger than he was.

"Okay class. Today we will delve into the beautiful world of upcycling. We've made art from feelings. Time to make art from trash. Pick something and get creating."

Todd waited for his classmates to choose before he ambled to the bin and grabbed an empty pop bottle. He stared at it, but no magnificent transformations occurred to him. Maybe some things were irredeemable. Maybe he was irredeemable.

"You don't think Claire will give me a second chance?"

Minh unwound the cardboard toilet paper roll she'd grabbed. "The redheaded chick who can't talk?"

"She talks fine." Todd surprised himself with his harsh tone. He was sick of people describing Claire as "C-c-claire," but he didn't have the right to defend her, even to her friend's little sister.

"Some people don't deserve second chances." Minh said as she attacked the cardboard roll with her art pens.

"How can you tell the difference between someone who deserves a second chance and someone who doesn't?" Cathryn said as she painted her washed-out potato salad container a bright orange. Her tone possessed a childlike innocence that suggested her question was genuine, but Minh shot her a glare as if they'd started an argument.

"Only decent human beings deserve a second chance." She grabbed scissors and snipped the ends of her roll.

Todd smashed the top of his pop bottle, but it did nothing to add to its aesthetics. "Okay, how do I become a decent human being?"

Minh looked like he'd just asked how to swim to the moon. "You want lessons?"

"Is that a thing?"

"No."

"I don't know, Minh," Cathryn said. "If you can turn a toilet paper roll into a dragon, can't you turn Todd into a decent guy?"

Minh unfurled her project, revealing an Asian-style dragon drawn in intricate detail along the cardboard coil.

Todd's jaw dropped. "Holy shit, that's amazing."

Minh tilted her head. "Lesson number one: Don't curse at a lady."

"You curse all the time, Minh," Cathryn said.

"Fine. Lesson one: Don't swear until you hear her swear."

"Okay," Todd said. "I can handle that."

Minh tapped her chin, warming to her new role as instructor in decency. "Lesson two: Take an interest in her interest."

Todd puzzled over that as he poked a pencil through his pop bottle, but Oliver appeared behind him before he could ask a follow-up question.

"What is that?" The teacher gestured to Todd's creation.

"It's, uh, symbolic."

Oliver drummed his fingers on his chin. "I see. The pencil represents the power of art to pierce through our definitions of trash and treasure."

"Sure, let's go with that."

Oliver grinned and, after gushing for several minutes over Minh's creation, turned to Cathryn's orange painted container.

"It's a traffic cone," Cathryn said. "A piece of trash is now a protective safety device."

Oliver sighed with enough exasperation to make a drama teacher proud. "My dear girl, somewhere inside you is a fierce artist. We just need to help her escape the boring librarian holding her hostage."

Cathryn's mouth dropped open in an appalled protest, but Oliver moved to the next table before she could voice it.

Minh laughed. Todd waited for her to finish before speaking.

"So my next step is to learn Claire's hobbies?"

Minh shrugged. "I wouldn't date someone who hated art, and if Cathryn ever pulled her head out of her books, she wouldn't date anyone with a vocabulary of less than a billion."

"The average college graduate has a vocabulary of only twenty to thirty thousand words," Cathryn said.

Minh held up her hands. "I rest my case."

Todd eyed his pencil-stabbed pop bottle. *I hope Claire isn't into art.*

CHAPTER 7

T odd snuck past his mother as she paced, phone to her ear, but her
angry voice carried.

"It's a photo of my body. I have every right to keep a copy, and I'll show
it to whomever I please, even if your face appears in the corner."

Some women ate ice cream after they got dumped. His mother
preferred blackmail. Todd pushed out the back door, trying not to think
about whether his past hookups had involved cameras, though it would
only matter if Claire gave him a second chance.

The air bit with a chill, warning of the impending frost. Todd would
harvest Old Man Caesar's crop later, but first he needed to help Noah
transition the greenhouse to hardier winter plants. The short walk
felt great on his stiff legs. Adam was networking, so Todd had taken
advantage of having sole possession of their room to study. Hours at his
desk only hurt his brain and stiffened his muscles.

The greenhouse's muggy air offered a return to summer. Todd
patched a few holes he'd spotted the last time he was here. Once he was
certain winter wouldn't breach the barrier, he pulled up the dead and
diseased summer plants and prepped the soil for the carrots, spinach, and
leeks to come.

By the time he finished, his muscles were stiff for entirely different
reasons, but he didn't return home. Some days, he wished he were Noah.
He'd spend whole days here, digging in the dirt, not caring about girls or
grades or gossip. At home, he spent hours studying and had nothing to
show for it. Here, he saw the fruits of his labor both immediately and at
harvest.

Claire likes to cook. Would she like some fresh vegetables? Minh had advised him to take an interest in her hobbies, and he already liked plants, especially the kinds he could smoke or eat.

As if hearing his thoughts, his stomach rumbled. Todd removed his gloves and wiped the sweat from his brow, wondering if Mrs. Thompson had felt well enough to cook today. Her chicken and dumpling soup beat the frozen burritos he had at home.

Fifi yipped, grabbed one of his gloves, and trotted toward the cash register.

"Fifi, no," Todd called, but she ignored him. Todd forced his tired legs to jog after her, but she moved fast for a three-legged dog. He crouched as he ran, trying to grab her, but he ran into someone's feet instead.

Todd scanned up, way up, until he met a hostile pair of eyes. Claire's friend Maite stood with Fifi in hand. The girl had caused more black eyes than any guy wanted to admit. She'd also warned Todd to stay away from Claire—before last year's drama. She must really hate him now.

"Absolutely not," said an older woman at the register, chatting with Noah as if WWIII weren't about to begin nearby. She shared Maite's gold-toned skin and black hair, but lacked Maite's height and Spanish accent. "I will pay full price, even if you haven't watered them today. I won't have it said I mistreat my providers."

Noah accepted her credit card. "You are my favorite florist."

The woman beamed, apparently not struggling to understand Noah's imprecise speech. "How is your mother?"

"The same. She liked the tea you brought."

"Good, because I brought more." She dug through a large canvas bag and handed some to Noah. "Like I said, add lemon juice and honey, and you'll never suffer a sore throat again."

The woman finished her transaction and turned, blinking when she spotted the two teens' silent glare-war. She cocked her head and regarded Todd, recognition in her eyes. No doubt Maite had told her about his role in the attack on Saafi.

The woman addressed Noah. "You do have a knack for working with strays."

Noah nodded and smiled at Todd.

Todd should have been offended—he helped Noah, not the other way around—but he couldn't muster negative feelings. Most people regarded him as a miscreant deserving discipline. It was refreshing, for a change, to be seen as a stray needing rescue.

Maite didn't share her relative's assessment, but she set Fifi on the floor and pulled their cart out the door. Todd gave Noah an update on his progress and fled, hating that school drama had invaded his sanctuary. He trekked home to meet up with Adam, forcing himself to look on the bright side.

He finally had something to contribute to his and Claire's economics project.

* * *

Todd sprinted to economics. His classmates gave him strange looks, but he didn't care. For once, he'd arrive on time.

He burst through the door a full minute before the bell rang, but Mr. Patel gave him a disapproving look.

"This is economics, not P.E."

Had he not been panting, Todd would have made a snarky comeback. He collapsed into his seat, gulping air and hoping his face wouldn't be beet red when Claire showed up. He'd just caught his breath when she and her friends strolled through the door.

Instead of her usual disapproving frown, Claire greeted him with wide eyes. *I guess that's an improvement.*

"You're early," she said as she slipped into the seat beside him. Her nose wiggled, not in the cute laughing manner, but in the something-stinks way. Todd recalled Cathryn telling him he reeked from smoking. His sweaty sprint wouldn't have helped. He'd have to make up for it with whatever charm he could fake.

Mr. Patel started class, giving Todd time to plumb the depths of his social skills for something that might please Claire. When the teacher at last released them to project work, Todd leaned back in his seat casually.

"I got something you'll like."

"I don't smoke," Claire said, deadpan.

Shit. He was aiming for "cool and intriguing," but he'd obviously misfired, wasting the preparation during Mr. Patel's droning. Off balance, his fingers fumbled his pencil, and it clattered to the ground.

"No, no. I have an idea for the project." He scrambled to retrieve his pencil, but bumped his notebook off his desk.

"Oh?"

"Yeah." He scooted closer to her and put his notebook on her desk, drawing as he spoke. "That farm-to-table stuff is popular, right? I figure we add a greenhouse to the restaurant and grow our own produce. We wouldn't need that much space if we opt for some vertical planters."

Claire leaned over his drawing, moving so close to him he smelled the strawberry scent of her shampoo.

"We'll nnnnnneed at least twelve square feet for a chicken c-coop."

"Chickens?"

"Fresh eggs," she said, as if this were obvious. "Just a couple, and just chickens. Roosters can be a pain. Also, I don't think corn can grow in a vertical planter, so we'll have to d-designate some ssss-space for a few rows." She added a square next to his.

"Well, we don't have to grow cor—"

Claire's glare shut him up. "Corn is a must." Her eyes grew distant. "God, I miss fresh corn."

Todd eyed their blueprints, which seemed to have grown into a micro-farm. "How did you become an expert on roosters and corn?"

Claire's expression suggested he was a moron for wondering how a Minneapolis teenager discovered roosters were a pain.

"I grew up on a farm in the middle of nowhere, Wisconsin." She exaggerated each word, though he suspected that was more to benefit his idiot brain than to prevent her stutter.

"Really?" Why hadn't he known that?

"Reed the rooster was my alarm clock. We had c-cows and everything." Claire leaned back, leaving him achingly aware of the empty air near him.

"Oh." Todd scrambled to recover from what he was sure Minh and Cathryn would label an obvious gaff. "So...you like my idea?"

"I love it." She spoke softly, as if loath to admit it. The bell rang, and she darted from the room, so keen to flee his presence she didn't even wait for her friends.

Todd reviewed that interaction throughout his next classes, but he couldn't qualify her running away from him as progress. By the last bell, he was dying for a smoke. Fortunately, he had a backpack full of the Ides of March to sell with Adam.

He navigated the twisty halls of the over-renovated school to the oldest wing. It had most recently housed home ec—before the program fell prey to budget cuts—but the wing must have served a dozen functions over the years. Rumors claimed the stoves still worked.

Todd rounded the corner, only to bump into Maite. She crossed her arms over her chest.

"Stay away from Noah."

"Believe it or not, I work at that greenhouse." The truth slipped out before he thought to lie. Hanging out with marigolds wasn't exactly good for his tough-guy reputation. Fortunately, Maite was no gossip. Unfortunately, she defended her friends with her fists.

She shoved him against the wall. "Noah is a good man. If you hurt him..."

"I would never hurt him, but I'll hurt you if you do." The scenario played out in his mind: Maite and her florist relative conning Noah into giving them a deal on flowers.

"I did not attack an innocent girl last year." Maite tightened her grip on his shoulder.

Todd wilted.

"Stay away from Clara," she said, using her nickname for Claire. She released him roughly and strode down the hallway, long legs taking her around the corner before Todd collected himself.

"Bitch," he said, but his stomach sided with Maite. His hope parasite drowned in the tumultuous acid her rebuttal had disturbed.

Todd strode to the old wing, needing a smoke more than ever. Adam, three guys, and a girl he didn't recognize leaned against the old sink stations.

"You're late," Adam said.

Todd threw his backpack to his brother, not in the mood to discuss what had delayed him. Money changed hands, lighters ignited, and soon Todd drifted in a pleasant high, oblivious to the surrounding conversation.

It wasn't until the guys departed that he realized he should have paid attention.

"See you tomorrow night," Adam said as he waved them out.

"Wait, what?" Todd said.

Adam laughed. "This is why I handle the business." He inhaled from his own joint. "We're meeting Joey at Old Man Caesar's to give him some Ides of March to sell, and he'll give us a discount on chalk. That way, we both expand our offerings."

"Speed? You want to sell speed? That's..." Todd trailed off. Marijuana was arguably innocent, but meth? They could go to jail for that.

"You should see your face." Adam laughed. "Relax, bro. I got a failsafe in case Principal Stick-Up-His-Ass decides to monitor us stoners. You just keep those thumbs of yours nice and green. I'll handle the rest."

Todd followed his brother to their car, thinking he'd rather use his green thumbs to grow corn and feed chickens.

CHAPTER 8

T he autumnal night's icy fingers clawed Todd's back. His breath fogged, and he mistook screeching brakes for a wolf's howl. He shook off his superstitions as their contact parked next to Old Man Caesar's. Adam's white teeth glowed within his grin as he shook hands with Joey.

Todd shivered, the cold stiffening his already sore muscles. He'd skipped school to harvest and process the marijuana before the early season frost. They'd doubled last year's harvest, so even after giving the boys their cut, Caesar had ample for himself. The old man agreed to continue this arrangement next year, expressing renewed interest in Todd's suggestion to add row covers to protect the plants from frost.

While Adam brokered the deal, Todd leaned against the car, aiming for a casual pose that wouldn't reveal his exhaustion. Next time, he'd tell Adam to handle the deal himself so he could go straight to sleep. Even if Adam needed him for backup, Todd would be more useless in a fight than a paper plane in a forest fire.

Gravel spat and popped down the road, no doubt another of Adam's contacts arriving. Todd raised his eyes to the sky, where the stars recorded the proceedings like a thousand camera lights. He wished he could skip school again tomorrow, but he didn't want Claire to think he was a flake.

"Who called the cops?" one guy shouted.

"You set us up!" Adam's contact shoved him to the ground.

The police turned on their headlights and blared the siren. The quiet, if eerie, night erupted into chaos. The guys scattered, tripping over one another as they fled to the woods. Todd hesitated, but the officers swept

47

flashlights around the grounds. He disappeared into the woods, running blindly until he stumbled upon a deer trail.

Roots grabbed at his feet and branches snagged his clothing, but he forced his fatigued legs along the trail to a clearing. A dumpster loomed like a hungry monster next to a large brick building. Several boxes lay folded in a neat pile beside it. Thinking he ought to hide, Todd dashed toward them. He picked one up, contemplating how to best build cover. The moonlight caught the label: LEWIS LIBRARY. Guess that explains Cathryn's obsession with books.

"Todd."

Todd whirled as Adam emerged from the woods like a shadow come to life. "You save the stash?"

"The cops won't care about a little weed," Adam said. His lower lip puffed out as if holding a grudge. "They will care about the chalk, which Joey still has."

He seemed upset, but Todd figured they'd dodged a bullet, literally.

"How long will they search before giving up?"

"We're small-time," Adam said, his tone indicating he'd like to change that. "They're probably already gone, but let's wait a couple of hours, just in case. Remind me to search the car for bugs and stuff before we leave."

Todd doubted the local police force would bug a teenager's car, but he didn't have the energy to object. He slumped against the library wall and prepared himself for a long, frigid night. *Looks like I'm faking sick tomorrow after all.*

* * *

Todd dragged himself into art. He'd tried to sleep yesterday, but his mother had spent the day screaming four-letter words through the phone. Her banker would need hearing aids after that conversation.

"Look who's back," Minh said.

Todd dropped into his seat and gestured to Cathryn. "Sorry."

"Sorry about what?" Cathryn asked. Todd squinted at her, but her face showed genuine confusion. She must not have been watching us. He blinked his bleary eyes clear. Was it just him, or was she wearing a lot more makeup than usual? Cathryn hadn't struck him as the Tina Lockard of the sophomore class, but maybe she was trying to burst free from her shy-girl cocoon.

Oliver instructed them to draw the next phase of evolution. Todd drew a stick figure of a guy with his eyes wide open, figuring he could say humans would evolve beyond the need for sleep. His thirty-second art project complete, he focused his energy on the upcoming economics class.

"How do you talk to a girl who's mad at you?"

"In the doghouse already?" Minh said as she added a cybernetic arm to the humanoid figure she was drawing.

"I'd advise an apology," Cathryn said.

"A little groveling never hurts either," Minh added.

"I don't grovel," Todd said.

Minh shrugged. "Your funeral."

Todd leaned his forehead against the table. Missing two class periods shouldn't be enough for him to lose his chance with Claire, should it?

"If I were to grovel, hypothetically, what's the best method?"

"You don't have to grovel," Cathryn said before Minh could answer. She, like Todd, had drawn a simple human figure and stopped. "Just be sincere about your apology."

"Yeah, but the apology only gets you out of the pit," Minh countered. "You'll need more than smooth talking to get invited to the penthouse."

"Like what?"

"Doing her favors, bribing her with gifts, planning a date..." Minh tapped her lower lip with her pen. "Whatever you do, don't start your apology with a compliment."

"Why not?"

Cathryn looked up from the book she'd buried herself in. "It will come across as trying to buy her forgiveness. Also, follow Benjamin Franklin's advice: 'Never ruin an apology with an excuse.'"

"Why are girls so complicated?"

Oliver reached their table before the girls could answer. He gushed over Minh's kickass robot chick and told Todd humans had already developed the ability not to sleep. Apparently, the teacher was a caffeine addict.

Oliver frowned at Cathryn's drawing. "That doesn't look very evolved."

"The next most likely evolutionary developments are things like an increased ability to multitask or greater resistance to blue light from screens," Cathryn said. "Nothing much will change to humans' exteriors. The idea that an increase in interracial marriages will lead to more people having beige skin tones represents a misunderstanding of the complex genetic factors determining—"

"Cathryn." Oliver closed his eyes and touched his pointer fingers to his thumbs. He stayed that way until the silence grew awkward. Cathryn looked at Minh, who shrugged.

He opened his eyes with a gasp. "In our next class, I want you to go wild, break all the rules. Break the very laws of physics!" He threw a fist to the ceiling and transitioned to the next table, leaving Cathryn confused.

Todd turned his drawing into a paper football, more to procrastinate crafting his apology than anything else. Minh held up her fingers in a goal post, and Todd shot it in, missing the days when he kicked real footballs. The bell rang, ending his procrastination. By the time he arrived, late, to economics, he was no closer to earning Claire's forgiveness.

Mr. Patel lectured on supply and demand curves, something Adam had a better handle on than Todd. For a change, Todd wished the lecture would last longer, but Mr. Patel released the class to project work before Todd finalized his apology.

Todd turned to Claire. *I'm sorry I ditched you for two days. I know this project is important to you, and I promise I'll make it up to you.*

"Uh, your hair looks nice."

"It's the same as always." She spoke in that exaggerated way that had the dual effects of preventing her stutter and making her sound like she was explaining something to an idiot.

Stupid, stupid, stupid. If Cathryn and Minh were correct, he couldn't apologize after a compliment. Maybe Claire would assume he'd been sick.

"I did some market research while you were gone," she said, placing particular emphasis on the last words. Todd grimaced, but she didn't accuse him directly. Instead, she showed him her notebook. "Land and overhead are expensive in the cities, and urban chicken coop laws are complicated. We may want to locate in a suburb."

A loud knock silenced the class. Two uniformed police officers strolled into the room, an odd-looking pair. The white guy towered over Mr. Patel, but his Latina partner barely reached his shoulder.

"Sorry to interrupt, Mr. Patel, but we're looking for Todd Easdon," the policewoman said, her voice deeper than her short stature suggested it would be.

Todd rose, his feet leaden. He looked at Claire, expecting an angry scowl, but she just wrote more notes, as if she'd expected to complete the project by herself. Her lack of faith in him hurt worse than her glares.

As Todd followed the cops to the office, his stomach roiled as if hungry wolves were tearing his hope parasite to shreds. Adam waited for them, leaning against the doorway.

"You won't learn anything else from him. It's like I said. We've never been to that house."

"Go back to class," the male officer said.

The two officers ushered Todd into the principal's office, where Principal Evans offered his chair to the female officer and took a seat beside Todd. The male officer stood, looming near the desk with his muscled arms crossed over his chest. His badge labeled him Officer Johansen.

"Your buddies from across town already ratted you out," the woman said—Officer Quintero, according to her name badge. "We know you were buying their products last night."

"No, I wasn't," Todd said. Technically, Adam had been the shopper.

Quintero leaned her elbows on the desk. "They specifically mentioned a stocky white male with short fingers on his left hand, and a twin."

"So?" Todd restrained a grimace as his voice rose to a squeak. He forced his nerves calm. "So a couple of guys have it out for us. Not like they're the only ones."

"We know it was you."

"Do you?" Todd said, relying on Adam's favorite fallback. "Did you see us there? No. You're relying on a drug dealer's testimony. Not exactly reliable."

Principal Evans cleared his throat. "I know you're on the honors track, Todd."

Todd blinked, brain scrambling to figure out why the principal mentioned that. "Even more reason to trust my word over theirs."

Principal Evans shook his head. "You have one foot on each path, but they're heading in opposite directions. If you continue this way, you'll tear yourself in two." His eyes held no condemnation. Rather, he looked like a father giving advice to his son.

Todd bristled at the presumption. "It's my life. Aren't you teachers supposed to foster independence or some shit like that?"

"Independence means making your own decisions. You can choose honesty, or you can follow your brother, but you may not like where he's leading you."

The words hit like a battering ram. Claire had said something similar last year. Then, he'd chosen wrong, but what was the right decision now? Turn in his twin, the only person who cared about him? Not a chance.

Todd lifted his chin and met Officer Quintero's eyes. "I wasn't buying anything last night, and neither was Adam."

Principal Evans stood. "Someday you'll have to decide what kind of person you want to be, Todd."

The officers escorted him out, and Todd's stomach loosened, but it ratcheted tight again when he spotted Cathryn waiting in an office chair.

"Come on in," Principal Evans said, gesturing for her to join them.

Todd's pulse roared in his ears as she disappeared with the officers. He feigned a casual air as he strolled out of the office, but as soon as he shut the door behind him, he paced, feet echoing in the empty hallway.

She would tell. Of course she would tell. She was one of those goody two-shoes smart girls like Saafi. Not only would she tell, she'd give them a detailed record of Todd's visits to her neighbor's garden, complete with the estimated height of the marijuana plants.

This is a disaster. All their careful planning ruined because of one shy girl with a conscience. What was the penalty for buying meth? Would the judge give him a warning, or would he spend the rest of high school in jail?

The bell rang, and students streamed out of their classrooms. Todd adjusted his pacing to weave around them, but made no moves toward his own third-period class. For once, passing time stretched too long. He thought he'd burn through his shoes before the halls finally fell silent again.

Cathryn emerged from the office, and Todd raced to her. He grabbed her shoulders, but she yelped and jerked away. She ducked out of his grasp and backed into the lockers across the hall, her chest heaving.

"Sorry." Todd held up his hands as he would when approaching one of Noah's rescue animals. "What did you say to them?"

Recovered from being startled, she scowled at him. "I know how to lie, Todd."

"You didn't rat us out?" A wave of relief pushed Todd against the lockers behind him. If he'd believed in God, he would have thanked him.

"No, but being good at lying doesn't make it right," she said, a pained tone in her voice.

"I'm sorry. We'll be more careful. It won't happen again."

Cathryn shook her head and stormed off, leaving Todd drowning in guilt. If the police caught them, would she get in trouble for covering for them? Was that what TV shows meant by "obstruction of justice?" It was one thing to risk himself—he had nothing to lose—but he didn't like the idea of hurting an innocent girl.

I need a smoke. The urge overwhelmed his senses, but his feet refused to carry him to the old wing. His pot smoking habit started this mess, and while he wasn't ready to quit, he couldn't bring himself to smoke right now. Neither could he go back to class. Instead, his feet took him home, past home, to the greenhouse.

Noah looked at him with surprise. "Don't you have school today?"

"Nope. It's a teacher training day."

Noah accepted the lie with a smile and directed him to set up the heaters they would soon need. Todd's guilt only increased. Lying to the cops barely tickled his conscience, but lying to the man who'd never wronged him? Principal Evans's words echoed in his mind. Todd certainly felt as if he were heading in the wrong direction.

Todd lost himself in manual labor, grateful Noah left him to himself. He worked until his arms felt like they would fall off. Unwilling to go home yet, he collapsed against the brick wall adjoining the greenhouse to the office. Would Noah notice if I slept here?

Fifi skittered over to him and sniffed. As if she'd smelled his despondency, she hopped into his lap and rested her head on his leg. Todd petted her, feeling more love from the dog than he'd ever received from his mother. Noah told him Fifi's previous owners were responsible for her missing eye and leg. Todd couldn't imagine unloading that much hate onto an innocent puppy. There were some lines even he'd never cross.

Then again, hadn't he already crossed them? What would happen to Cathryn if the police caught them? What had already happened to Old Man Caesar? At the very least, the police had harassed him. After that debacle, Todd doubted the old man would let him continue working his marijuana plot, but as he petted Fifi, he couldn't muster any disappointment.

He didn't need to grow marijuana to feed his smoking habit. He could find another source, and he could satisfy his green thumb helping Noah. No more risking innocent people.

His conclusion drove the anxiety from his body, and he drifted off to sleep.

* * *

Todd's muscles ached worse than after football tryouts. He shifted, but a knot in his neck muscles restrained the movement. Wishing he were still unconscious, Todd opened his eyes.

He would have thought Noah and Mrs. Thompson would have sent him home, but someone had draped a homemade quilt over him. Todd's chest ached at the tender gesture. His own mother wouldn't have done that, not that he deserved the kindness.

He checked the time on his phone. The light filtering through the greenhouse had woken him early. He had plenty of time to run home and shower before school, assuming he wanted to return to school. Yes. Fatigue may have muddled yesterday's thoughts, but they'd been genuine. He'd play it straight from now on, starting with an apology to Cathryn. And Claire.

Todd took his time walking home, enjoying the dawn of a new day. His mother and brother were still asleep, so he luxuriated in the shower long enough to soothe his sore muscles. With yesterday's unpleasantness scrubbed clean, he felt like a new person, a better person.

"Where were you last night?" Adam greeted him with a cheeky grin.

"With a brunette." The lie slipped past his lips without a thought. So much for playing it straight.

"Told ya you'd get over that redhead." Adam's grin widened as he pushed past him toward the shower. Guilt flashed through Todd for having drained the hot water, but he dismissed the feeling. Adam hadn't harvested or helped with any other manual labor in their operation. Todd deserved a hot shower for his work.

If Adam was upset about his cold shower, he didn't show it. He dropped Todd off at the side entrance before parking in their usual spot. Todd jimmied his way through the door, grateful he no longer had to endure his former teammates' scorn as he entered the building. Their hatred ate away at him, though Adam fed off it. Sometimes Todd wondered if they were opposites rather than identical twins.

Todd strolled into art, barely on time despite his early start. Minh glared at him as if she'd evolved her cyber chick's laser eyes.

"Decent Human Being Lesson Number Four: Don't Do Illegal Shit."

"What did he do?" Cathryn asked. The innocence in her tone brought Todd to a halt. She looked as if she genuinely had no idea what Minh was referencing; a performance so flawless, Todd wondered whether he'd imagined their conversation from yesterday. After he confirmed his memory, his gut twisted. Should he be taking lessons in decency from someone so skilled at lying?

"You need to pull your head out of your books, Cat," Minh said, oblivious to her friend's deception. "Todd here got away with selling meth, right under the police's noses. Word is he has an oil drum full of pseudoephedrine hidden in his basement."

"I'd have thought you were too smart to listen to gossip," Todd said as he took his seat.

"That is gossip." Minh pointed to the Gossip Girls, who giggled, ponytails wagging as they whispered. "I am well informed."

"*Mis*informed."

Oliver started the lesson before Minh could respond. Todd ignored her attempts at communication for the rest of class. He didn't even glance at whatever amazing art thing she'd created. As soon as the bell rang, he shot out the door and booked it to economics.

People said redheads had tempers because of their hair, but it was Claire's eyes that burned with green fire.

"Nice of you to t-t-take time off from your life of crime."

"I..." Todd's jaw waggled up and down. "I can explain. It was a misunderstanding."

"Sure. Just like last year."

Todd's eyes involuntarily drifted to Saafi, who feigned interest in her planner. Her face was grave with memory, but she held her silence.

"Claire—"

"Sssstay away from me. I'll d-do the project by myself."

Todd sank into the seat beside her. He'd begun this day thinking he'd become a new person, but he'd encountered nothing but reminders of the old one. Starting over wasn't as easy as Principal Evans made it sound. You couldn't forge a new path when the old one trapped you in quicksand.

Todd spent the rest of class staring into space and longing for a cigarette. *What am I supposed to do?*

CHAPTER 9

Todd snuck through the kitchen, but an argument blocked his route to the stairs.

"You can't stop supporting your sons," his mother said.

"But I can stop supporting you." His father handed her an envelope. "This is all the child support due until they turn eighteen."

His mother snatched the envelope. "It's not enough."

"The judge will disagree. I'm telling my wife the truth, so don't even think about demanding more." His father left with his shoulders straight, relieved of the weight of two teenage boys.

His mother screeched and whipped out her phone, scrolling with a frenzy as she paced the living room. Todd waited until her back was turned before dashing to his room.

"How is dear old Dad?" Adam asked without taking his gaze off his phone.

"Officially not responsible for us anymore. He paid Mom for the rest of our childhood."

"How will she fund her next face lift?" Adam's tone was dry, as if he were too bored to inject sarcasm into his statement.

Todd plopped onto his bed, but his marigold plant's drooping leaves gave him the plant equivalent of sad puppy dog eyes. He'd been so quick to criticize Fifi's former owners, but he couldn't even care for a plant.

Todd reminded himself marigolds were annuals. Their winter deaths were inevitable, but he couldn't help wondering whether it would have lived longer if he'd tended it better. It sat on his shelf, abandoned.

He averted his gaze. Was this why his father stalked them from a distance instead of getting close? Could he not bear to see the reflections of his own failures? Or did he simply not care about Todd and Adam? How else could he enjoy being free of them? Todd felt more guilty about his dying marigold than his father did about his struggling sons.

"Forget them," Adam said, gesturing to the wall. Next to his alien-eyed picture of their father's family was a newer portrait. This time, Adam had pierced their eyes with pins.

Todd leaned against his pillow, carrying all the weight his father wasn't. Adam eyed him, then strode to their closet and pulled out an old box.

"You think this thing still works?" He held out an old video game console, a relic from one of their mother's past boyfriends. Todd had been sorry to see him go, but his start-up hadn't proved as profitable as his mother had hoped.

"Come on," Adam said. "Let's try it out."

Todd would have preferred to sulk, but he appreciated Adam's trying to cheer him up. He followed his brother to the basement TV. Their mother was AWOL, but they wrestled the wires by themselves and hooked up the console.

They'd perfected the art of throttling each other with animated avatars. With every virtual blow Todd landed, the real-life wound his father had dealt healed a little more. Soon they were laughing, enjoying a night of innocent fun like normal kids with a normal childhood. Todd could almost imagine his mother calling down the stairs to say dinner was ready, and they'd better finish their homework before they played anymore.

Todd landed a fatal blow. "Yes!" He raised his arms in victory.

Adam shoved him. "I'll get you next round." His phone buzzed. He broke into a grin and jumped to his feet. "We have a Halloween party to crash."

Reality crushed Todd's victory. Couldn't they just pretend to be normal for one night?

"I'm not in the mood."

"Yes, you are," Adam countered. "This is more than a party. It's damage control."

Todd stood. "You still want to deal? Can't we just...I don't know, slow down?"

"Slow down? No. We can't slow down. I want out of this hell, don't you?"

"Yeah, but—"

"You think Dad has a college fund for us?"

"No, but—"

"Mom doesn't give two shits about us. Nobody does." Adam's eyes softened. "It's us against the world, bro."

Todd ran his thumb along his stubby fingers. Adam was right. Their father wouldn't help them. School wouldn't help them. They'd be lucky if their mother didn't sell their organs. They were on their own, but at least they had each other's backs.

Todd nodded at his brother. "Let's go."

* * *

Todd groaned as consciousness teased him. He felt as though his body were wobbling within a giant bowl of gelatin. Everything was numb, yet everything hurt.

"This isn't a good idea." The voice had a familiar feminine tone, but Todd couldn't place it.

"Relax, I'm almost done," another girl said. I know who that is. It's... His brain overheated trying to identify the speaker. Something scratched his arm. What the hell?

He cracked his eyes open, regretted it, and squeezed them shut again. Someone giggled. Todd prepared himself for daylight's cruel bite before opening his eyes.

Minh smirked beside him, pen in hand.

"Wha?" Todd's sluggish tongue couldn't finish the word. He didn't remember coming to school. He hadn't planned to, not after last night. At the party, he'd drunk and smoked and slept with a girl whose name he didn't recall. She'd grimaced at his short fingers. That, he remembered.

Whiskey shots had soothed his hurt feelings, so when she'd failed to find a more attractive partner, he'd eagerly accepted her offer to "make it up to him."

That was all he remembered.

"How...?" He sleepwalked sometimes. Had the alcohol triggered an episode? He and Adam drove to school, because anyone with a car drove, but they lived within walking distance.

"Welcome back to the land of the living," Minh said.

"Do you need the nurse?" Cathryn's face filled with concern. "You look...green."

"I'm fine," Todd said, closing his eyes. This wasn't his first hangover, and school wasn't the strangest place he'd woken up in after a sleepwalking episode. When he was eleven, he'd awakened in an igloo the neighborhood kids had constructed.

Cathryn didn't look like she believed him, but Oliver approached before she could reply.

"And what do we have here, artists?"

"Cathryn thought we should expand beyond the bounds of traditional media, and Todd volunteered himself as a—what did you call it, Cat? A biological canvas?" Minh gestured to Todd's arm.

Dread slowed Todd's head-turn, and when his eyes found his arm, his brain didn't believe them. A fire-breathing bunny now graced his forearm, complete with a rainbow tutu.

"Right on." Oliver nodded at Cathryn. "That's the spirit." He moved to another table, and Cathryn's eyes widened.

"That was not my idea."

"I didn't think it was," Todd said. He'd be more upset if Minh weren't such a talented artist. That bunny could defeat a battalion of super soldiers. "This isn't permanent, is it?"

"Relax, it's just pen." Minh waved a dismissive hand as the bell rang.

Todd stood, struggling to keep his feet. He staggered to the nearest drinking fountain and guzzled water for several minutes. Once sated, he started for home, but his legs carried him in the opposite direction.

He knew it was a mistake the instant he crossed the threshold into economics. His classmates stared. Even Mr. Patel, who usually waved latecomers to their seats without stopping his lecture, opened his mouth in stunned silence. Todd still wore his nicest party clothes, but he must look as hungover as he felt. He probably smelled like it too.

"Doesn't the dress code require tattoos be covered?" someone in front asked.

"It's not a tattoo," Todd said before Mr. Patel could answer. "It's just Minh's prank."

"Minh? As in my sister Minh?" Beth shot out of her chair like a pouncing cat, uncharacteristic intensity contrasting her usually dry tone. "What were you doing with my sister?"

Todd held up his hands. "We have art together. I fell asleep, and she doodled." He realized, belatedly, that he was humiliating himself, but the honors crowd already considered him a deadbeat. Impressing them had never been Todd's goal. He'd wanted to impress Claire, but even if the meth lab rumors hadn't turned her off, this incident would.

"Todd Easdon to the office, please," the static-filled intercom commanded. "Todd Easdon to the office."

Mr. Patel waved him away as if he were brushing crumbs off his suit coat. Todd stumbled to the office, wondering what other trouble he'd caused himself while sleepwalking. The school secretary didn't bother looking up from her computer before waving him into the school counselor's office.

Mrs. Moore greeted him with a curt nod, but her face shifted to uncertainty as she scanned his rumpled appearance.

"Todd," she said. "Do you feel safe at home?"

"What? Oh." He grimaced, recognizing the expression teachers used when they thought they might need to report abuse or neglect. Todd and Adam learned early that rumpled clothes and lack of showers led to questions, and the last thing they wanted was Principal Evans meeting their mother. "Yeah, I'm fine."

The kindness melted off her face. "Good." She dropped a file in front of him with a thump. "You're failing your classes. Time to drop honors." She handed him a half-sheet of paper. "Here is your new schedule."

Someone knocked before Todd could process her words. Principal Evans stuck his head inside.

"May I borrow Todd for a moment, Mrs. Moore?"

Mrs. Moore waved Todd out, as if grateful to be rid of his stench. Todd followed the principal into his office and slouched into an open chair. What now?

"Todd, I'd like you to stay in the honors classes."

"Huh?" Todd was too stunned to form a complete sentence. He must still be asleep. That was it. He was still at the party, passed out next to that girl.

"Good party last night?"

"Yeah," Todd said, struggling to follow the dreamworld's conversational whiplash.

"Worth the hangover? You feel fulfilled, appreciated, and respected?"

"Huh?" Todd couldn't keep up with the principal's words. Was the party worth the hangover? Of course. Wasn't it?

Todd considered that, grateful the principal didn't seem to expect much from him this morning. At the party, he'd pushed aside all thoughts of being "decent." After weeks of striving to earn a smile from Claire, a prettier girl had slept with him, but he'd woken up sick and...he couldn't identify the feeling, but it certainly wasn't "fulfilled, appreciated, and respected."

"You feel empty, don't you?" Principal Evans watched him with knowing eyes.

Todd started picking the dirt from beneath his fingernails. Empty was exactly how he felt, how he'd felt ever since Claire dumped him, ever since he'd helped Adam see Saafi's hair. Partying had been like funneling water into a bucket with holes in it.

"You're capable of more than hangovers, Todd." There was that tone again. That fatherly tone Todd so loathed.

"What do you know?"

"I know you signed yourself up for the honors track. I'm guessing you did it for a reason."

"I did it for a girl." Todd's tone was so bitter the words were brittle.

Principal Evans nodded, as if he hadn't expected that answer but was willing to roll with it. "I take it she doesn't find hungover, racist ex-jocks attractive?"

This was the first time the new principal had alluded to last year's drinking fountain incident, but his tone lacked accusation. He spoke as if relaying the facts, as if he were saying Todd was a seventeen-year-old guy of stocky build.

"You could be someone people admire," Principal Evans said.

"You have a redemption quota?"

The principal refused to match Todd's aggressive tone. "I offer all my students a second chance, including your brother, but you are the one I think will take me up on it." His voice dropped to a near whisper. "Don't waste your life being a coward, Todd. Figure out what you want, and fight for it."

One word—coward—echoed in Todd's skull, dragging him back to last year when Claire dumped him. *"You're a coward, Todd...I hope you learn to sleep at night."* He hadn't. Maybe he never would.

Todd sprang to his feet, fists clenched. "You don't know shit about me, and I don't give a shit about your second chances."

"Then why are you crying?"

Todd wiped his cheeks. He hadn't realized his eyes were leaking. "I'm hungover."

Principal Evans stood and stepped toward him, but he stopped short of putting his arm around Todd. Good. Todd would have clocked him.

"I'll tell you what. Stay in the honors courses. If you want to be a professional drunk, it won't kill you to flunk, but I think you'll rise to the challenge. You may have joined for a girl, but you'll stay for yourself."

Todd averted his gaze. No one had ever voiced such confidence in him. No one had ever suggested he might succeed where Adam had failed.

"Am I excused?"

Principal Evans nodded. "Go home, shower, and decide who you want to be when you're eighty."

Todd didn't think about anything more than trudging home. He pinched himself. It hurt. He pinched himself again with similar results. For good measure, he raked his nails against his skin until he bled. It hurt. He must be awake.

He let the shower rinse off the blood, spilled booze, and Minh's penned tattoo, but the water couldn't wash away his conversation with the principal. A conversation he hadn't dreamt.

Adam snored from his bed, confirming they'd made it home last night. Todd dropped into his own bed, but his mind wouldn't let him sleep.

What kind of person do I want to be when I'm eighty? He'd never even considered life after high school, much less his elder years.

Todd wasn't naïve enough to believe they'd become infamous drug dealers or gang lords or whatever Adam had in mind. With his current trajectory, Todd would become Old Man Caesar. He considered this outcome. The guy grew good weed and spent all day smoking it. He didn't have to work or bother anyone. Sounded relaxing, especially compared to the constant activity in teenage life.

Caesar also lived in a dilapidated shack on a gravel road to nowhere. Alone. If teenagers didn't pester him for pot, he could die, and no one would realize it until archeologists dug up the site a hundred years later.

Is that the life I want? Todd's eyes strayed to the family photos his brother had mangled. He didn't want to become his father. Whether he died young on the streets or lived to be a crazy old pothead, he would never become a man who abandoned his sons. Do I even want kids?

Todd swung his legs over the edge of the bed and squinted at the photos. His father looked happier than Todd ever saw him, especially in the second photo where the kids were older. He held Shanice's hand, his white fingers intertwining with her brown ones.

Todd had kissed his fair share of girls, but holding hands implied a level of emotional commitment he'd never permitted. If he'd learned anything from his mother, it was that sex was cheap, but love required trust.

A scene popped into his mind—an older couple holding hands and wandering through the grocery store. They'd been married so long they didn't need to talk, but they spoke anyway because they enjoyed hearing each other's voices. The idea stirred up foreign feelings in Todd, a desire that grew stronger the more he pondered it. He wanted a relationship that lasted longer than one night, with a girl whose name he remembered. He wanted to stay with the same woman so long his hand felt empty without hers. Nothing could be further from his current life, nothing less attainable.

Todd gazed at his stubby fingers. Would he ever find a girl willing to hold his left hand? How many heroic stories would he invent before he found someone who accepted him?

Claire wouldn't care about my fingers. He knew that like he knew plants needed water, but Claire hated him.

Todd glanced at his backpack, which he'd left behind in his sleepwalk to school. Mrs. Moore hadn't officially kicked him out of the honors track. Was it too late to earn Claire's trust? What was the alternative? Becoming everything Mrs. Moore thought he'd become.

No. He wouldn't settle for the life everyone expected for him.

Todd grabbed his backpack and tiptoed out of their bedroom to avoid waking Adam. He settled himself on the living room floor and opened his economics book. The terms in bold may as well have been a foreign language. Graphs splattered the pages like hieroglyphics. Every paragraph was heavy with words too big for a normal human to pronounce. His other textbooks proved equally inaccessible.

The hours ticked by. Todd rubbed his bleary eyes, but it did nothing to make the text more decipherable. His stomach rumbled. Was it too early for lunch?

His mother pushed through the front door, tripped, and cursed. She shot Todd a glare.

"Adam, I told you not to leave your shit everywhere."

"I'm Todd, Mom. Shouldn't our own mother be able to tell us apart?" Usually, she could at least accomplish that level of parenting.

"Well, you can't blame me." She gestured toward his books. "It's not like you've ever been the brainiac."

True. Adam was the criminal mastermind; Todd, the lackey. Even with school, Adam never studied because he never had to study. Socializing came easier to Adam, too. They were supposedly identical, but Todd suspected his brother had stolen all the good genes in the womb and left him with scraps.

Todd's expression must have reflected his thoughts, because his mother's face softened. She tottered over the carpet in her high heels and crouched in front of him. Todd recoiled from her outstretched hand, but she merely patted his cheek.

"You know I love you, right?"

No. "Yeah."

She smiled as if he were a baby she were trying to make giggle. "Take my advice and focus on these muscles"—she poked Todd's biceps—"instead of this one." She patted him on the head and stood. "You're a man. You'll make an easy living if you can lift heavy things. Be grateful. Women need brains." She puffed out her chest as if alluding to her "creative" entrepreneurship. "I have a lunch date. Clean up before I get back."

She flounced out the door, leaving Todd in a storm of emotion. Were he in calm waters, he would have been offended by her implying manual labor wasn't hard work, but a tidal wave of shame swallowed him. What if she was right? He'd never been as smart as Adam, and Adam had left the honors classes. He'd have dropped out entirely if school weren't his primary networking locale.

Todd swallowed a lump. Even if he dropped the honors track, he'd still fail. Not only was he an idiot, he was a coward. Even Principal Evans had noticed Claire wasn't attracted to "hungover, racist ex-jocks." His own father didn't think him worthwhile. Why should Claire? Why should any girl?

Todd's chest constricted until he couldn't breathe. He left his books to rot by the sofa, crashed through the back door, and ran, legs pumping out his feelings. His feet crunched over fallen leaves until he entered the greenhouse's humid microclimate. He breathed deeply, but the earthy smell didn't comfort him like it usually did.

Todd collapsed where he'd slept the other night. Only after Fifi started licking his cheeks did he realize he was crying. Great. I can't even be the tough guy.

He brushed away Fifi's attention, petting her before looking around. Noah leaned against a plant stand, watching him. Seeing he'd been noticed, he plopped next to Todd. His jaw wiggled from side to side, as if he were composing his next words carefully.

"High school sucks," he said.

"You're telling me." Todd hugged Fifi. Noah remained silent, making Todd wonder how his high school days had been. He'd always envied Noah's quiet life, but high school must have been hell for someone whose diagnosis announced itself on his face.

Todd's friends teased Claire for stuttering, even though she was smart, even though you'd never guess judging by her appearance. People rarely teased Todd about his fingers, but they did stare at them. Even when handing him change, people avoided touching him, as if he'd lost his fingers to a disease that would transmit through his stubs. How much worse had Noah's childhood been?

"People suck," Todd said, knowing he had to include himself, the cowardly idiot, in that group.

"Some do, but they don't matter." Noah stood. "You can sleep here whenever you want, but let me know because if it happens a lot, I will have to make you a really big doggie bed." His grin made Todd chuckle, and once he started laughing, he couldn't stop. Noah joined him with an unashamed belly laugh that echoed through the greenhouse.

Nothing changed, but Todd felt better anyway.

"Do you want some soup?" Noah asked, gesturing toward the house.

"Yeah," Todd said, and somehow, he knew he'd be okay.

CHAPTER 10

Todd rushed to the art room, hoping his good night's sleep at the greenhouse would help him make sense of his economics book. Oliver instructed them to "use black and white to evoke the colors of emotion," and directed them toward a bin of charcoal. Todd drew a squiggly line and returned to his book, a strategy that worked better for him than for Cathryn.

His well-rested eyes read the words, but the extra sleep hadn't boosted his brainpower as much as he'd hoped. He tried focusing on the graphs and charts, but even those eluded him. Maybe his mom was right. He didn't need a big brain to hold a girl's hand, right? Would big muscles impress Claire?

Probably not. Todd returned his focus to the textbook, but he only retained a tenth of what he read. He shoved the book aside and muttered, "I'm an idiot."

"Yeah you are," Minh said. Todd shot her a glare, but she cut him off. "You're struggling through a textbook by yourself while you have a human encyclopedia sitting next to you." She gestured to Cathryn, who looked up from her book.

"What?"

"I'm not asking a sophomore for help with my homework," Todd said.

"Then you're even dumber than you look, because Cat is the smartest girl in school."

"That's an exaggeration," Cathryn said.

Minh shifted her reproving gaze to Cathryn. "You have a photographic memory."

"Is that really a thing?" Todd asked.

"Technically, no," Cathryn said. "But it is a colloquially acceptable description for a variety of memorization techniques that allow a person to retain a prodigious amount of information."

Todd understood only half the words in that sentence, but he guessed that was Minh's point. He pushed his textbook to Cathryn.

"Prove it."

She scanned the page, then handed the book back to Todd and recited the passage verbatim.

Todd's jaw dropped. "That's insane."

"Told you," Minh said.

"I'm best with history and English," Cathryn said.

"But she'd rather salivate over the big words in your economics textbook than explore the essence of charcoal," Minh said as she added more strokes to her drawing.

Cathryn nodded, and Todd found himself with a sophomore tutor whose entire body weight would equal his left thigh but whose brain was the heavyweight champion of academics. She broke down the concepts into digestible pieces, and Todd learned more in twenty minutes than he had in his hours-long study session.

"Drawing in your textbooks?" Oliver said. "I like it."

Todd and Cathryn exchanged a nervous glance.

"No," Minh said as she slid her drawing across the table. "This is our offering for the day."

Todd gaped at the picture. She'd captured Todd's dejection and drawn an eager-looking Cathryn peering over his book. Detail that good should have taken weeks to craft.

"Excellent work, Minh, as always, but I'll need Todd's and Cathryn's art too."

"Prioritizing individual contributions is a Western cultural construct," Cathryn said, syllables spilling out of her mouth even faster than usual. "Other cultures emphasize collectivism. Collaboration is an important skill to develop for the workplace, especially with the rise in globalization resulting in more cross-cultural interactions."

Oliver stared at her as if she were speaking a foreign language.

Minh held up her hands as though receiving a blessing from the heavens. "We allowed the inspiration to flow from their brains through my fingertips, and we hope the result will inspire art lovers the world over."

Oliver nodded. "Right on. Keep up the good work." He moved to another group.

"That doesn't even make sense," Cathryn said once Oliver turned his back.

Minh smirked. "That's the point, Cat. Didn't he tell you to break all the rules?"

The bell rang. Cathryn shook her head and followed her friend. Todd must have walked with an extra-large spring in his step, because he arrived at economics on time.

He sat through Mr. Patel's lecture, remembering Noah's words when his classmates snuck glances at him and whispered. They don't matter. When Mr. Patel released the class to project work, Claire scooted closer to her friends, making it clear she neither expected nor wanted his help.

Todd refused to let her rejection dampen his good mood. He reviewed the content Cathryn had taught him, knowing Claire would only accept his help if he knew what he was doing.

The girls started whispering, and the whispering led to chatting. Todd eavesdropped just enough to confirm they were comparing projects and not ridiculing him. Mr. Patel strode toward the group, hard-soled shoes clacking on the classroom floor.

"Ladies, I expect you to work on your own projects." He directed the comment to Claire.

Todd cleared his throat. "Prioritizing individual contributions is a Western culture thing. Other cultures emphasize, uh, collectivism. With the economy being more global and having cultural contact and stuff, it's good to, uh, collaborate and...you know." He'd been so sure he'd remembered all of Cathryn's big words, but his academic pontificating fizzled beneath his classmates' critical stares.

Mr. Patel pinched the bridge of his nose as if warding off a migraine. "Just work on your projects."

He left to answer another student's question, but Beth, Saafi, and Claire still gaped at Todd. After an awkward silence, Saafi broke into soft giggles, which she covered lest Mr. Patel hear.

Todd's mouth dropped open. Saafi hadn't smiled in his presence since last year, but now she was giggling. His hope parasite warmed within him.

Beth and Claire were not so easily amused.

"What. Was. That," Beth said.

"Did you swallow an encyclopedia this morning?" Claire said.

Beth slapped her desk, as if Claire's comment clarified everything. "You've been hanging around Minh's friend, haven't you?"

"Well..." Todd searched for a plausible lie that didn't involve revealing he'd asked a sophomore to tutor him.

Beth's gaze hardened. "I thought I told you to stay away from my sister."

"Technically it was Cathryn—"

"I don't approve of you spending time with her either."

"Hey, I'm not a—" He almost said monster, but Saafi was looking at him, big brown eyes waiting for something. An apology?

Todd hung his head. "I'm just trying to finish high school."

"So you asked a sssophomore for help?" Claire said.

"I didn't ask. She offered." More like Minh volunteered her, but she hadn't objected.

"If you needed a tutor," Saafi said, "why not ask one of us?"

"No," Beth and Claire said simultaneously. They shot Saafi a warning look, and Todd had to agree with them. If Saafi thought to offer herself as a tutor, then she forgave too quickly.

"Cathryn is skittish as a baby rabbit, but she makes Einstein look like a moron." Beth leaned forward. "You put one finger on that girl, and I'll tell Maite to rip your arms off."

She won't need to ask Maite. If Maite's reaction to seeing him at the greenhouse reflected her opinion of him, she would jump at the chance to pummel Todd.

"I'm just trying to finish high school," Todd repeated, hoping to end the conversation by returning his attention to his textbook. The girls left him alone, but the bell rang before he made any headway into the next chapter.

"Claire?" he called as the room emptied.

Claire lifted a hand to stop her friends from following her back to Todd's desk. Todd couldn't imagine having friends so loyal he needed to signal them not to help.

"Yeah?"

"You don't, um...You don't think I'm a worthless idiot, do you?" He finished the question with his eyes.

Claire perched on the desk, holding his gaze. "I went to sssssss-speech therapy for thirteen years. I'm not ashamed of asking for help, and you shouldn't be either. Besides,"—her gaze drifted to where Minh's bunny drawing had graced his arm—"looks like you need it."

Todd wasn't sure whether to consider today a success. Claire had surmised his life was a mess, but she hadn't told him to leave her alone. Was that progress? He wouldn't have thought admitting his weaknesses would earn Claire's esteem, but Minh and Cathryn had recommended sincerity. Maybe they were right.

Todd gathered his books and headed to his next class. *Girls are weird.*

CHAPTER 11

Todd slammed his civics book shut, but Cathryn, vicious task master, didn't acknowledge his tantrum. She grabbed a hunk of clay and broke it into twelve parts.

"These represent citizens of two electoral districts." She put the lumps on a piece of scratch paper and drew a line to separate them. "Each group has four Republicans and two Democrats." She drew an R or D under the respective lumps. "If the Democrats redrew the district line like this"—she separated off the Democratic lumps—"they would win that district. That's gerrymandering."

"You just redraw the lines so your party wins?"

"You got it," Cathryn said.

"Politics is disgusting," Minh said as she snatched one of their clay lumps.

"True, but it's easier to play the game if you know the rules," Todd said. High school worked the same way. With Cathryn's tutoring, his grades had risen a full letter. Not that moving from D's and F's to C's and D's would impress Claire, but it was a start.

"Speaking of games"—Minh grabbed another lump of clay and shaped it—"how goes your quest to win fair redhead's heart? Beth is grouchy, so I assume it's going well?" Her tone didn't reveal her own opinion.

"I think your sister hates me more for talking to you than for working with Claire," Todd said.

"I can take care of myself." Minh squished a lump of clay as if to demonstrate what she'd do to Todd if he misbehaved. "Now answer the question."

Todd shrugged. "Claire talks to me now, only about our econ project, but that's better than cursing my name."

Minh frowned as she smoothed an angle on her clay figure. "Have you tried bribery?"

"Minh," Cathryn said.

"Cat, how many of the books you've read were romance novels?" Minh's tone suggested she already knew the answer.

"None," Cathryn admitted. "I suppose there is an established historical practice of men buying flowers and chocolate during courtship."

Minh gave Cathryn the look she used when threatening to drag the bookworm out of the library more often, then turned her attention to Todd.

"Skip the flowers, but your gift should involve chocolate. Unless she has a known allergy, in which case you're doomed."

Minh returned to sculpting, but Todd couldn't focus on Cathryn's lesson. What would Claire like? He pondered Claire's tastes, dismayed by how little he knew. She played volleyball, grew up on a farm, and wanted to open a restaurant. Flowers and chocolate didn't seem likely to win her favor.

"Cat, do you think I need another guy here?" Minh asked.

Todd gaped at Minh's creation. She'd taken the lumps Cathryn had used to represent electoral populations and turned them into soldiers on a battlefield, complete with tortured facial expressions.

"Is there any form of art you haven't mastered?" Todd asked.

Minh shrugged. "I prefer ink pens, but clay feels nice between the fingers." She raised her eyebrows at Cathryn.

"You only ask my opinion so you'll have an excuse to enact the plan you've already made."

Minh nodded as though Cathryn had given her a real answer. "You're right. The soldiers are perfect, but the tank needs some damage." She pressed her finger into its side, creating a realistic dent.

Oliver gushed over the display. "Art has always played an integral role in war. Just look at Guernica." He showed them the painting on his phone, but Todd preferred Minh to Picasso.

Oliver's fingers fluttered as if he were sprinkling fairy dust over the group. "I'm getting wonderful vibes from you three. Keep it up."

Todd chuckled on his way to economics and brainstormed gift ideas during Mr. Patel's lecture. He observed Claire, hoping for inspiration. Perhaps his crush warped his perspective, but she looked especially pretty. Even without any insight into women's fashion, he could tell her green sweater flattered her. It was loose enough to accommodate her muscular arms, but hugged her torso enough to reveal her fit form. When she faced him, green eyes bright, Todd couldn't breathe for a few heartbeats.

She handed him a sheet of paper. "I drafted the menu last night. I'll have to compare suppliers and plan a b-b-b-budget before adding the prices, but since you've developed an interest in 'collaborating,' you may as well take a look."

Todd perused the menu. "Don't you think people will want soup while it's cold outside?" He always wanted soup, but maybe his experience with Mrs. Thompson's homegrown vegetable soups skewed his objectivity.

Claire snatched the paper from him and chewed the end of her braid as she scanned it. Stupid. Stupid. Stupid. Insulting the judgment of the girl you wanted to date had to be number one on Minh's list of mistakes to avoid.

"You're right." She flipped open her notebook and jotted notes. "We need more c-comfort foods, and we should rotate the mmmmenu to feature seasonal dishes."

"You're not mad?"

Claire furrowed her brow. "Why would I be upset with you for having a good idea?"

Girls are so weird. When Todd tried to be smooth, he angered her, but when he acted like an idiot, she empathized. When he complimented her, she took offense, but when he insulted her menu, she praised his ideas. Puberty must rewire girls' brains into nonsensical tangles.

The rest of the day passed with blessed mundanity. Thanks to his art class study session, he breezed through his civics quiz. Adam snuck him an extra chocolate milk at lunch, and his math teacher gave them the night off from homework. By the time he transitioned from autumn's chill to the greenhouse's summery humidity, he was humming a cheerful ditty like a cartoon character. Except the cartoons usually fall off a cliff afterward.

Todd pushed his foreboding aside and checked the heaters, reminding himself to tell Noah to buy a backup generator in case they lost power. Otherwise, the plants would freeze.

As if summoned, Noah appeared beside him. "Can you man the register? Mom is having a rough day." He gestured to the outside, implying the cold didn't help her health. "I'll be back soon. I just need to check on her."

"Sure." Todd strode through the greenhouse to the office/shop/register. Noah moved beyond that and into the house.

Todd scanned the surroundings, but Noah had already cleaned. With nothing better to do, he made a list of seasonal vegetables for Claire's menu.

A bell chimed. Todd's gut clenched as two women in hijabs entered, but they didn't recognize him.

"Where is Noah?" the taller one asked.

"Checking on his mom," Todd answered, knowing the Thompsons were open about her health problems. "I can help you."

The woman pursed her lips as though considering waiting for Noah. "I have an order under the last name Xoriyo."

Todd was grateful she spelled it, because the pronunciation didn't lend itself to easy interpretation. He had enough trouble with his civics vocabulary, much less Somali names. He found her order in the system and retrieved her box of broccoli and kale.

"We don't need the box." The shorter woman lifted an intricately woven, yet sturdy, bag onto the counter and loaded it with the vegetables. Todd blinked. Claire liked to cook, and cooking required shopping, right? Would she like a bag?

He cleared his throat. "Um, do you mind my asking where you bought that?"

The shorter woman raised her eyebrows.

"I mean, for my girlfriend," Todd said quickly. If Claire heard him refer to her as his girlfriend, she'd give him a bloody nose, but the explanation made the woman's eyes twinkle.

"Midtown Global Market."

"Thanks." Todd accepted their payment and took their order for the following week, feeling odd after they departed. Saafi was a popular girl, so after last year's incident, he'd rarely interacted with Somalis who didn't want to tear his guts out. He'd almost forgotten normal human interactions—just a greenhouse worker helping a customer. It felt good to serve instead of scheme.

The bell chimed again, but this time it wasn't a customer.

"Keep those green thumbs limber," Adam said without introduction, "because we are back in business."

"What do you mean?" Todd glanced toward the house, hoping Noah wouldn't walk in on this conversation.

Adam leaned against the counter like he owned the place. "I sweet-talked Old Man Caesar into letting you tend his plot again this summer. We'll need an alternate location for deals, but I'm working on that."

The news threw Todd's feelings into a maelstrom. Caesar's yard had been his own personal heaven last summer, but he'd hoped to escape the trouble it brought and spend more time in the greenhouse. If it were just the Ides of March, Todd wouldn't mind being involved, but marijuana wouldn't satisfy Adam's ambition. He wanted the power dealing harder drugs would bring, and as last year's quest to see Saafi's hair proved, he wouldn't hesitate to hurt innocents to get what he wanted.

"Speaking of"—Adam handed Todd a wad of cash—"here's your cut from the deal we did at the party."

Todd's stomach lurched. He'd rather forget that party, but he remembered the Somali woman's bag. Such a gift wouldn't come cheap. He wasn't sure how Minh's decency scale would rank purchasing a present with drug money, but she couldn't object if he invested in a local business, right? At least he wasn't buying more drugs.

Todd pocketed the cash. Adam grabbed a rake and twirled it.

"By the way, we're meeting Joey on Friday."

"I can't," Todd lied. *I'm not selling anything more than the Ides of March.*

Adam dropped the rake. "What do you mean you can't?"

"I have a date."

"With who?"

"None of your business."

Todd's nose didn't need to grow for Adam to see through his lie. Fortunately, he missed the bullseye.

"It's the redhead, isn't it? God, Todd. Can't you see she's using you?"

For what? Todd kept his thought to himself, but the door chime ushered in more trouble.

Maite ducked inside. As soon as Adam spotted her, he picked up the rake, brandishing it defensively. Maite positioned herself between him and her relative, who had entered after her.

Todd lifted his hands. "Hey, let's not make trouble for Noah."

Maite stood her ground like a medieval tower with all its cannons pointed at Adam. Adam feigned a jab with the rake, but before the two could brawl, Noah returned from the house. He smiled as if he'd caught them playing pinnacle instead of fighting.

"Ms. Rojas, nice to see you. I have your order ready."

Maite's relative scooted out from behind Maite and approached the counter. Todd still hadn't figured out the relationship. The woman's face sported enough lines to be Maite's young grandmother, but her hair was still jet black, so she could be an older mom. Aunt?

"How is your mom?" Ms. Rojas asked.

Noah grimaced.

"I thought so." She dug in her bag. "I brought her some homemade *ajiaco*. Nothing like homemade soup on a frosty night."

My thoughts exactly. Todd relinquished the register to Noah and joined his brother, who was still brandishing the rake. Maite looked unimpressed.

"Jorge dropped out of school."

"And we care because?" Adam said.

"He is my neighbor. His mom said he smokes all day." She turned her dark eyes on Todd. "Because of you, yes?"

Adam lowered his voice so the adults wouldn't overhear. "You want to fight, bitch? Because you're outnumbered."

Maite smirked as if she liked her odds, which she probably did. Last year, she'd defended Saafi against three guys by herself. She widened her stance, but Ms. Rojas called her.

"Let's go. We have vegetables to cook."

Maite turned her gaze to Noah. "You should buy security cameras. They help with people like them." She jerked her head toward Adam and Todd and followed her relative out the door.

Adam's face twisted with disgust as he put the rake away. "Bitch."

"Don't think about her. We got Old Man Caesar back on board, and you have another deal."

Adam glared at the door. "Yeah, you're right." He turned to Todd. "Enjoy your date, bro. I'll handle Joey." His scheming look destroyed any comfort the words brought.

"Maite is friends with the cops, remember?" Todd wasn't sure that was true, but the local police unit sponsored the Brooks High volleyball team, so he assumed they were at least on good terms.

"You're right." Adam clapped him on the shoulder. "Maite's not worth the trouble." He didn't bother waving goodbye to Noah before leaving.

Todd helped Noah close, but boulders sank in his stomach. He wasn't as good at reading lies as Adam was.

Chapter 12

The second he set foot in the Midtown Global Market, Todd questioned the sanity of going this far to buy a present for a girl who hated him. The smells hit first—spicy, sweet, sour, savory—like the whole world shoved up his nose in one breath. After that, the colors assaulted his eyes. Bright patterns decorated the open-concept mall where vendors hawked everything from groceries to clothing to jewelry.

Todd had never felt so lost.

When he'd asked the customer where she'd bought her purse, he'd assumed Midtown Global Market was a small shop, not an entire universe in one building. If the sights, smells, and crowds hadn't already disoriented him, the cacophony of foreign language banter would have.

He stood smack in the middle of the aisle between vendors, a cactus in the rainforest. Even though his summer tan had lingered, compared to the rest of the clientele, his skin appeared as pale as the gamer dorks who hunched over their laptops all day. This was a bad idea. Todd turned to leave.

"You've got a lot of nerve showing up here," a Somali girl he vaguely recognized from school said. She widened her stance: feet set, arms spread apart from her body as though trying to make herself bigger.

In other circumstances, her spunk would've amused him—he could easily toss her over his shoulder—but the environment unsettled him, and he was trying to stay out of trouble.

"I was just leaving."

"You're lucky Saafi is—"

"Todd?"

Todd whirled to see Saafi approaching from the bathroom.

"What are you doing here?" she asked.

"Nothing." A crown of sweat formed along Todd's hairline. "I was just leaving."

He pivoted, but the crowd prevented him from power walking to the exit.

"Todd." Saafi's voice called him closer, but her body shifted away from him. She linked arms with her friend, who scanned their surroundings as if searching for backup. "Why are you here?"

Todd made the mistake of meeting Saafi's eyes—the deep brown, compassionate eyes of a girl he had so utterly wronged. As always, they waited for an apology, one he couldn't give without acknowledging his and his brother's guilt. Even so, the words "I'm sorry" lodged in his throat, aching to be released. The least he could do was answer her question.

"I...I saw a girl with this cool bag, and I thought Claire would like one."

"You're trying to win her back," Saafi said. "You weren't a good influence on her."

Todd scuffed the concrete floor. "Maybe she'll be a good influence on me."

"It's not her job to fix you," Saafi's friend said, her tone less charitable than Saafi's.

"Falis is right. It's your job to prove yourself."

"Why do you think I'm here?" Todd's patience frayed. Everyone told him to "be better," but when he tried, they threw up barriers. "Look, I get it. I shouldn't have told everyone Claire slept with me." That, at least, he could apologize for. "But how else can I make it up to her?"

The girls stared at him. Someone bumped into Todd. He stepped forward to avoid getting hit again, but the girls retreated, pushing against a table. Todd shifted sideways, allowing them an escape.

"You're really sorry?" Saafi asked. Todd sensed she was talking about more than his false rumor.

"Yes." He said it forcefully to erase any doubt of his sincerity.

Saafi met his gaze, searching his eyes for an apology to her? "Okay, we'll help you find something."

"What?" Falis said. "No. No-no. I am not using my shopping superpowers to help him."

Saafi squeezed her friend's arm. "Think of the challenge, Falis. I mean, who could be less qualified to buy a woman's purse than Todd?"

"Actually"—Todd cleared his throat—"I was thinking more of a shopping bag. You know, for vegetables and stuff? Because Claire likes cooking. Right?" Todd didn't have asthma, but the spiced air scratched his lungs—that or his nerves. Regardless, the sensation triggered a powerful instinct to flee, but Saafi was right. What did he know about girl stuff?

Saafi and Falis gave him that weird look girls give small children when they've done something too cute to punish. Falis raised a finger.

"I still think you're worse than the scum that congeals around the bath drain, but Claire is okay, and I know where to find the perfect bag."

She led the way, weaving through the crowd. Todd's bulky build hindered his progress, and she drummed her fingers together while waiting for him to catch up.

"What's our budget?" Falis said.

"I've got the cash." Todd decided not to expound on exactly how much money he had and how he'd obtained it. They might rescind their help if they knew. Besides, it wasn't as if he was saving for retirement.

Saafi chuckled. "You're going to regret not giving her a budget."

Falis grinned wickedly.

The girls examined several beautifully woven but stiff textured bags, debating the merits of each. Load capacity, strap size, interior pockets, buttons vs. straps vs. zippers—Todd hadn't realized buying a bag was so involved. If women's clothing was this complicated, it was no wonder girls spent so much time shopping. In the end, they decided on a medium-sized bag, concluding Claire would want fresh enough produce to warrant shopping often.

Falis eyed his wallet as he paid the vendor. "Business is booming in the old wing, eh?"

"What makes you—"

"Relax, Todd," Saafi said. "I may be a goody two shoes, but I'm not that naïve. At least you're spending it on a good cause." Her smile cracked something in him. The gesture was so...sweet, especially compared to his mother's scowls. Could he get Claire to smile more? Or better yet, laugh? He loved the way her nose wiggled when she laughed, but it had been a long time since he'd seen that.

Falis tapped his shoulder. "We're not done."

"Huh?"

"You can't give a girl an empty bag," Saafi said, as if that clarified everything.

His continued confusion must have shown on his face, because Falis's wicked grin returned.

"The bag is merely the vessel for the other presents your weed money will buy."

"Spices," Saafi said. "Claire loves spices and herbs. Come on, I know a place with quality cardamom."

Apparently, Saafi knew not one, but three places to buy spices and herbs, but even that wasn't enough to complete his gift bag. The girls dragged him around the market, zigzagging between various shops. Todd wasn't sure if they just enjoyed shopping or if they considered spending his money to be some type of revenge, but he didn't care. If his gift made Claire smile, it would be worth it.

"Our work here is done," Saafi said as she added a scented candle to the bag. "Claire will love it."

"Of course she will. I'm a professional." Falis's eyes lit up. "What if I were a professional shopper? There must be a huge untapped market of helpless men needing to buy their girlfriends' forgiveness." She turned to Todd. "Would you write a customer testimony for me?"

"Uh, sure." Todd examined the wares. They looked like a pile of random stuff to him, but the girls dubbed it a masterpiece.

"I make no guarantees that Claire will forgive you," Saafi said.

"I should put that disclaimer on my website," Falis said.

Saafi laughed and hooked her arm through Falis's. "Come on, I'll help you start your business plan."

"Saafi?" Todd called after her. "Why did you help me?"

Her face fell, as if she'd needed his reminder that she wasn't supposed to like him. "We can't undo last year, but we can make this year better. If helping you makes you think twice before doing something hateful, then it was worth it."

Falis, also reminded she hated Todd, tugged Saafi away before they could speak more.

"Thank you," Todd called after them, wishing he'd said, "I'm sorry."

CHAPTER 13

Oliver had already started class when Todd arrived. Not wanting to explain the bag to Adam, Todd had made up an excuse to walk to school, but he'd misjudged the commute.

Minh raised an eyebrow. "Didn't take you for a murse kind of guy."

"It's for Claire. You told me to get her a gift."

The other eyebrow joined the first. "I told you to get her a chocolate bar."

"I did." Todd showed her the three gourmet chocolate bars he'd bought.

"Such a...generous offering may come across a little strong," Cathryn said. "Isn't this for a first date?"

"For a first date, it's way too heavy-handed, but..." Minh tapped her paintbrush against the table. "For an apology, you may need more."

"What?" Todd said. He'd spent well into the triple digits on this gift bag.

"Didn't you tell everyone Claire bit you in bed?"

Todd groaned. He'd been trying to explain his split lip, unwilling to admit Maite's fist had done it.

"It's a good first step," Cathryn said. "You're partners in economics, right? Ask her on a study date."

"Not everyone considers studying a date, Cat," Minh said.

"Exactly. Claire can spend more time with you without committing to romance."

Todd mulled that over. "I guess that makes sense."

Cathryn smiled her triumphant-shy-girl smile. "Speaking of studying, don't you have a biology test this week?"

Todd laid his head on the table. As if navigating relationships weren't hard enough, his grades sailed through rough waters. He pictured Claire's laugh, with her cute bunny nose wiggle, and lifted his head.

"Yeah, let's get to it."

Cathryn took all of five minutes to learn his biology content. Knowing her, she'd studied in her free time, which was good because Todd needed a lot of help. When the bell ended their study session, he was reasonably confident he'd pass.

Whether he'd pass Claire's test was another matter.

"Here. This one should be dry enough to add to your gift basket." Minh handed him one of her watercolors. Her other painting—various sports balls arranged into the Olympic rings—had earned the praise "ringing in global harmony" from Oliver. "Beth loves these, so I figure Claire will too."

Todd examined the multicolored volleyball painting, certain Claire would love it.

"Thanks."

His classmates gave him strange looks as he hauled the bag down the hallway, but he was used to attracting attention. Whether he was sprinting to get to class on time, or hungover with a bunny drawing on his arm, he couldn't seem to avoid being gawk-worthy. He decided he didn't care. The gossips weren't his friends, but Claire might be more than a friend if his plan worked.

Mr. Patel released the class to project work early, so Todd arrived late enough to miss the entire lecture. He took a deep breath before entering the classroom, reminding himself that Falis and Saafi's help hadn't come with a guarantee.

Saafi gave him an encouraging wink, but Beth and Claire gawked as he set the bag on Claire's desk.

"What. Is. This."

Todd palmed his neck. "You don't like it? Saafi said—"

"Saafi helped you with this?"

Saafi spread her hands. "He let us shop without a budget."

Claire stood, eyes flaming. "I c-c-can't believe you'd T-ake advantage of her like that."

"She offered, and didn't you say I shouldn't be ashamed of needing help?"

"I..." Claire's mouth wobbled open, but none of her speech strategies could help her if she had nothing to say.

Mr. Patel cleared his throat. "If you won't work, take your drama outside, and expect a detention." He returned to his desk, and their classmates sheepishly abandoned their spectating.

Claire dropped into her seat with a huff. Todd lowered himself more gently into his.

"I'm sorry for spreading rumors last year. I know you hate me, but I want to help with our project."

Claire sniffed the spice-filled bag and peeked inside. "Did you get cardamom? The g-g-good kind?"

"Saafi assures me it's the best in the Twin Cities." Todd was suddenly grateful they'd investigated three different spice shops.

Claire buried her head inside the bag, sniffing as she sifted through the spices, herbs, candles, and other girly things.

"Strawberry-scented lotion doesn't make up for last year," she said, clearly referencing all of last year.

"Is it enough to let me work on our project? If it has my name on it, I should help." Todd wasn't sure whether to apply the same principle to Minh's artwork. Baby steps.

Claire found the chocolate bars and grinned. "I guess so."

A semester's worth of tension whooshed out of him. "Great. Since I'm behind, do you want to work after school? Together?"

Her eyes hardened at his hastily added last word. "Are you asking me on a d-d- D—are you asking me out?"

"No." Todd held up his hands.

"Good, because my answer would be no." She sniffed the spices, and the anger drained from her face. "Okay. I need to cook with these. You can help me test the menu."

"I'm free tonight," Todd said, thinking he may not have lied to Adam about having a date after all.

Claire inhaled the spiced scents again. "I'll text you my new address."

CHAPTER 14

Todd's insides shivered as much as his outsides as he traversed the frosty sidewalk to Claire's apartment. Nerves had never plagued him before a date, probably because he'd never been on a proper date. Sure, Adam had arranged outings, but Todd had always approached them intending to make out with the girl—or more, if possible. Most girls loved big biceps, so Todd was an easy sell, especially if alcohol was involved. Now, however, he wanted Claire to like him, not just his muscles—a feat so difficult he wondered why guys bothered bragging about their sexual conquests. The relational ones were a much bigger challenge.

He buzzed the intercom for the apartment listed under Peterson, and the door clicked open. He climbed to the third floor and knocked, hands sweaty despite the chilly weather.

Claire opened the door, and classical music drifted from inside. "You came."

"I said I would."

"Your word isn't a guarantee."

Todd shifted his weight. "I hope to make it one."

Claire hesitated before waving him into an apartment that was a perfect balance of comfortable and formal. Not a speck of dust rested on the shelves, but the modern-style furniture showed signs of being well-loved, especially the chair by the window. Quality appliances filled the small kitchen, where Claire had already laid out the ingredients. The only threat to the apartment's feng shui was the photographs decorating the walls and shelves. All of them looked as if they'd been taken within the last year.

Todd examined a group photo. He recognized Claire and her teammates, but the setting was unfamiliar. The sun set over a grassy field, and a barn stood in the background. An older couple bookended the group, presumably Claire's grandparents.

"They had trouble accepting my city friends," Claire said. "Thought they were a b-bad influence. Turns out you were the bad influence."

"Sorry," Todd murmured, wondering how he could become a decent human being when everyone kept reminding him how awful he was. Saafi had helped him, but she had the most right to hate him. Crazy upside-down girl world.

Todd scanned the room for a change in subject and gestured to her stereo. "Do you always listen to Beethoven when you cook?"

"That's Bach," she said, sounding more offended by his lack of musical literacy than his bad influence. "But if you prefer..." She pushed a button on the stereo, and music with a driving beat sounded through the speakers.

Todd tapped his foot to the rhythm. "Cool."

"Cumbia is Maite's favorite," Claire said as she moved toward the kitchen.

Todd hesitated, unsure whether he was allowed to like the same music as Maite. Deciding that was too complicated a question to answer right then, he followed Claire.

She gestured to her assembled ingredients. "We're making b-butter and herbed roasted chicken with Cajun spiced mashed sweet potatoes and crisp mmmmaple brussels sprouts."

"Sounds delicious," Todd said. And like a lot of work. Not that the workload mattered. The longer the meal prep, the more time he could spend with Claire.

"It's a p-p-perfectly balanced meal," Claire said as if she doubted Todd's sincerity. "It has sssssssavory, sssss-spicy, and sweet flavors and incorporates a variety of food nutrient groups."

She preheated the double oven and placed a thawed chicken in a roasting pan, but when she pulled out a huge knife, Todd glanced around.

"Wait, we're doing this by ourselves?"

"My grandparents live three hours away, and Aunt Monica burns pasta."

"Is that even possi—"

"Yes. Trust me. We're b-better off on our own." She pointed the knife at him. "But don't get any ffffffunny ideas. Maite taught me self-defense."

Todd lifted his hands. "I'm just here to make chicken."

"Good." Claire slit the chicken's skin. "To start, we rub the butter and herb mixture beneath the skin." She grabbed a glob of butter, shoved it beneath the chicken's skin, and looked at Todd. "Didn't you say you wanted to p-participate more?"

"Oh, right." Todd was used to getting his hands dirty, but getting them slimy with butter and chicken juice was a novel experience. Claire stuffed the butter in a smooth layer. Todd's butter clumped, and he broke through the skin in places.

"Here, like this." Claire grabbed his hand and used it to rub in more butter, but Todd couldn't focus on her technique. Noah's three-legged dog gave him kisses, but he couldn't remember the last time a human being did more than clap him on the shoulder. Claire's touch was appropriately casual, but to him, it felt magical.

She released him, leaving only the sensation of slimy butter coating his fingers.

"Right," she said as they washed their hands. "Now into the oven, and we ssssstart chopping vegetables."

Todd tried to match her expert knife work, but he was better with a shovel or spade. She instructed him to make all the slices the same size, but his clumsy cutting made that impossible.

"I'd better be careful, or I'll cut off the rest of my fingers." His joke fell flat. Claire peered at his hand, as if just noticing it. Instead of looking away, as most people did, Claire set it on the skinned sweet potato and covered his knife hand with hers. She was standing so close her body heat warmed him.

"Angle the knife away from your fingers, like this." Claire helped him chop. "Got it?"

"Yeah," Todd said, though the strawberry scent of her shampoo had made paying attention impossible. She returned to her side of the counter. She couldn't stray too far in the small kitchen, but she stood much farther than Todd's body wanted.

Cool it, Todd. He needed to use his head, but another part of his anatomy was staging a coup. He set the knife aside and scanned the room for a distraction.

Why would she put a photograph next to the sink? Wouldn't it get wet? Todd shifted his position to see better. At first, he thought of the family portraits Adam had vandalized, but Claire's was pin-free, the only old photo he'd seen in the apartment. A round-faced redheaded woman and a dark-haired man with a pointy chin hugged Claire in the family closeness Todd had always wanted. Claire had experienced it and lost it. Was that better or worse?

"What happened to them?"

Claire's knife froze halfway through a potato. "They're dead."

"I figured," Todd said before he thought better of it. "Sorry, I—"

"It's okay. We were in a c- c- motor vehicle accident, hit a d-deer on the highway. Mom died at the scene, and Dad..." Her eyes went dull.

Todd kicked himself as he remembered Saafi telling him about her father's suicide. "I'm sorry."

"I found him." Her lower lip trembled, but when he reached out to her, she held up her chef's knife. Todd backed away. Stupid. Stupid. Stupid. Way to ruin everything.

Claire cleared her throat, but her words emerged a whisper. "Let's just cook."

Grateful she hadn't thrown him out of her apartment, he returned to chopping, but the casual atmosphere had vacated the room. Claire popped the potatoes into the second oven and started slicing the brussels sprouts in half, but Todd could only stare at the little green balls beneath his four stumps.

"It was an infection," he said.

Claire looked up from her cutting board. "What?"

"My fingers. I injured them when I was ten, and it got infected. They had to amputate before I lost my whole hand."

"I didn't ask for an explanation."

"I know. That's why you deserve one." He wouldn't delve into how he'd injured his fingers, but after making her relive her parents' deaths, he owed her some honesty.

Claire returned to her chopping. "That's silly. I don't d-deserve anything for not being a Gossip Girl."

"Maybe so, but you were the first girl to choose me over Adam. That's worth something." Todd picked up his knife, but the round brussels sprouts proved even trickier than the potatoes.

Claire took his knife away and chopped his share of the vegetables. "You were the ffffirst guy I met who didn't c-care about my stutter." She piled the brussels sprouts onto a tray and mixed the glaze. "The first, but not the only. Kyle Rogers asked me out."

"Kyle Rogers?" Had Todd been holding his knife, he would have dropped it when he pictured Claire with the lanky, pale-faced kid who looked like a twelve-year-old but dressed like a seventy-year-old. "But he's so boring."

Claire laughed. "He d-doesn't eat anything. The guy is vegan, gluten-free, and allergic to nuts. He ssssspent the entire date lecturing me on why cheese is the root of all evil."

"What did you do?"

Claire drizzled the glaze on the brussels sprouts and popped them into the second oven with the sweet potatoes.

"I showed up at his house the next d-day wearing my cheesehead and a T-shirt with my grandparents' dairy farm logo on it."

"You didn't."

"Yep."

Todd laughed. "I can imagine his face. Wait, do you still have the cheesehead? Can I see it?"

Claire put a hand to her chest. "Asking to see a girl's cheesehead on a study date? Isn't that a little b-bold?"

"Not as bold as wearing it to a vegan's house."

Claire chuckled and dashed down a hallway. A moment later, she returned with an enormous foam block of cheese on her head. Her smile blossomed as she twirled.

"How do I look?"

Like the most beautiful girl I've ever seen. "He didn't ask you on a second date?"

Claire laughed and tossed the cheesehead on the couch. The room filled with the scents of home cooking, and Todd's stomach growled. After the timer finally rang, they blended the spiced sweet potatoes with some chicken broth. His stomach growled again, and Claire poked him.

"Don't you eat at home?"

Not if I can help it. "We mostly eat frozen pizza."

He thought he'd receive more teasing, or even a lecture, but Claire nodded. "After Mom d-died, I ate cereal for dinner a lot. That's why I lllllearned to cook, and why I want to open a restaurant someday. Cooking saved me." She barely moved her lips when saying her last words, and they emerged as a whisper.

"That's a good reason." Todd wished he had a bigger vocabulary to express how much he admired Claire's life plans. He didn't have goals, but he would gladly support the dreams of this volleyball-playing, dairy-loving orphan from Wisconsin.

The thought sobered him. Claire's dreams hadn't interested him last year. He hadn't even known her mom had died, much less that she loved to cook. When they'd been fooling around, he'd focused on himself.

"I was an ass," Todd said.

"Yep." Claire grabbed a chef's knife and started carving the chicken.

"An apology isn't enough, is it?"

"Nope." Claire twisted the chicken leg, cracking the hip joint as she ripped it free. A single knife cut separated it from the thigh.

"Is making chicken always so violent?"

"You wouldn't last a d-day on a farm." Claire repeated the process with the other leg and finished carving, arranging the meat on a platter before rinsing her hands.

"I don't know. I mean, I like plants."

Claire paused on her way to the cupboard. "What?"

Todd's cheeks warmed. He hadn't realized he'd said that last sentence out loud, but maybe he could salvage the interaction.

"I work at a greenhouse."

"You work at a g-greenhouse? One that grows vegetables?"

93

Todd held up his hands. "I may be missing fingers, but I have two green thumbs." He stepped toward Claire. Had she retreated, she would've wedged herself into the corner between the cupboards and fridge, but she stood her ground, as if challenging him to try something stupid.

Todd opened the cupboard above Claire and grabbed some plates. "And both of my green thumbs would be happy to help you set the table."

Claire smiled and reached past him to the silverware drawer. He stood still, and she didn't push him away. Her arm was so close to touching him that his skin tingled.

She grabbed two forks and knives and closed the drawer. "We can eat now. I nnnnnever know when Aunt Monica will get home."

Though the apartment boasted a small dining table, they elected to eat at the counter. Todd's eyes rolled back in his head as he tasted the chicken.

"Oh my God." He shoveled more into his mouth before forcing himself to exercise restraint. Probably wasn't best to eat like a pig in front of a lady.

Claire giggled. "Yeah. That's how I fffffffelt last year. After weeks of cereal, Saafi invited me over for dinner. Her aunt's surbiyaan is amazing."

Todd swallowed before speaking. "Saafi is...way too nice."

"You're t-t-telling me. She's nnnnnever had a drop of alcohol, or even dropped the f-bomb." Claire shook her head. "She makes me feel like a terrible person."

"Glad I'm not the only one."

Claire stared at him for an awkward moment. Todd took a bite, which seemed to break the spell. They finished the meal in an amicable silence, which Todd appreciated. It allowed him to fill his mouth with food.

Not wanting the evening to end, he insisted on doing the dishes while she set aside a serving for her aunt and put away the leftovers. Claire set the empty tray in the sink and touched his arm. He looked up to find her earnest green eyes evaluating him.

"I don't know what to do with you, Todd."

"Give me a second chance?"

"No." Claire held out a set of disposable food containers filled with leftovers. "B-but I will give you the opportunity to earn a second chance."

Fireworks exploded inside him with such force that it took him a moment to realize the containers were for him. A thousand socially acceptable responses flashed through his mind—thank you; I didn't expect leftovers; I enjoyed our dinner—but his mouth stuck open.

He reached for the containers, hands resting on hers. They were warm, and he longed to hold them there. He ached to draw her close, kiss her, hold her, and never let go.

The door burst open. Todd yanked the containers out of Claire's hands, fumbled them, but controlled their fall to the counter. In walked a woman who must be Aunt Monica even though she looked nothing like Claire. Rather than Claire's round face and curly red hair, she had black, stick straight hair and a face full of sharp angles that cut into Todd the moment she saw him.

"Isn't that—"

"Yes," Claire said.

The woman slung a large purse onto a waiting coatrack. "You didn't tell me he was your econ partner."

"I was just leaving," Todd said. He shot Claire a quick smile, grabbed the containers, and headed toward the door, but Monica blocked his path.

"You do anything to hurt my niece, and I'll make the chicken's death look merciful." She moved out of his way, shoved him into the hallway, and closed the door behind him.

Yikes. Despite the unfriendly reception, he couldn't muster any discouragement. Claire was always surrounded by bodyguards—Beth, Saafi, Maite, and now her aunt. Frustrating as they were, he was glad she had so much support. He'd only ever had Adam.

Todd trudged into the dark night to the bus stop, but the cold didn't chill him. Claire said she'd give him a chance to regain her trust. That was warmth enough.

When he arrived home, he dropped straight into bed, full in more ways than one. He dreamed of working on a farm, tending plants all day, and eating roasted chicken in the evenings. He must have still smelled the chicken odor on his clothing, because the dream was delightfully real, but Adam's cursing ripped him out of it.

"That bitch!" Adam paced in front of his bed.

Todd blinked from groggy to wakeful. "Huh?"

"Maite. It had to be her who called the cops tonight." He paced, eyes dark, scowl so deep it looked like it carved his face down to the bone. "We'll get her. Oh, we'll get her good."

Todd's good feelings evaporated, and suddenly he was cold. Cold and empty.

CHAPTER 15

Once again, Todd dressed in black, covered his face, and snuck out with Adam, but now, Todd felt like the older brother. These pranks had ceased entertaining him last year, and he was as tired as an old geezer who didn't bother scaring kids off his lawn anymore.

"Are you sure it was her?"

"You saw her at Noah's. She blamed us for her neighbor dropping out. That's motive." Adam glanced around the corner before facing Todd. "Are you backing out on me?"

"I just—"

"It's Claire, isn't it? God, Todd. Don't be such a dimwit. That girl will drop you the second you become inconvenient. She's no better than Mom. No girl is."

"That's not..." He stopped short of saying "true" because he was teetering on the edge of Claire's good graces. One wrong move and she would leave him, as everyone did. Everyone except Adam.

"The cops drew their guns. I don't care if Maite is friends with your crush. We could have been killed. If we don't teach her not to meddle in our business, she'll ruin us."

Todd rubbed his stubby fingers. Adam had dragged him to help when he'd been too feverish to think straight. He'd saved Todd's life. Assisting with minor vandalism seemed small compensation.

"Okay, we'll send her a message, but let's make it quick." He had a civics test tomorrow, and he couldn't afford to sleep through his art class study session.

They scanned for trouble as they wove through winding back alleys, but not a soul ventured out into the cold winter night. By the time they reached their destination, Todd's fingers and toes had numbed. He wondered, idiotically, whether that would affect his spray painting, but no one cared whether vandals wrote neatly.

Flores de Fernanda stood two stories tall, with Maite and her relative living in the upper apartment. The glass gleamed, clear despite the dirty slush that contaminated everything during the winter. They must wash it regularly. Todd cupped his hands around his eyes to peek through. Though the darkness hid the details, the florist's shop was tidy and clean, organized to optimize the displays in the small space. Todd admired the maintenance work. Ms. Rojas obviously took pride in her work.

Adam spray painted a penis over the flower bouquet in the logo. Todd added a few sloppy f-bombs, frozen fingers unable to hold the spray nozzle well enough to maintain a constant paint stream.

He couldn't help thinking of all the hours he'd spent wiping smudges off the greenhouse's front door. Noah had once asked him to repaint it after they'd changed hours, and it had taken an entire day to achieve a professional look. Todd cringed as he added the word bitch to the side. Maite had hours of scrubbing in her future.

"Okay, are we done?"

Adam paced in front of the window.

"Adam, let's go."

"No." He grabbed a slush-covered rock. "I'm sick of her smug mug showing up everywhere." He chucked the rock, but it bounced off the window, leaving a small chink.

Adam growled and stalked into a side alley where a dumpster lay. He ripped off a piece of a crate and swung it like a bat, but the wood splintered on impact, leaving the storefront intact. Adam tossed the remaining half aside.

Todd grabbed his arm before he returned to the dumpster. "Adam, that's enough. Let's clear out before they wake up and call the cops."

"It's not enough." A deranged look overtook Adam's face, stunning Todd into loosening his grip. Adam charged into the alley and returned carrying two broken bricks.

"Adam, don't." Todd placed himself between his brother and the storefront. Spray paint was one thing, but exposing those delicate flowers to the wintery weather? Even Noah's hardy vegetables wouldn't survive that.

"Move," Adam said.

Todd held his ground, but Adam stalked around him. He threw a brick, but Todd intercepted it. His momentum carried him past his brother, and Adam hooked his foot around Todd's ankle and yanked. Todd landed in the slush, and Adam hurled the other brick through the glass.

An alarm blared.

"Shit." Todd scrambled to his feet.

Adam acted like he didn't hear. He kicked a bigger hole in the glass, retrieved the brick, and threw it through another portion of the window.

Todd dragged his brother away from the scene. Adam struggled, but unlike Todd, he hadn't been doing manual labor after quitting sports. Todd pulled him through the winding alleyways until he was certain no one pursued them.

"What the fuck, man?" Adam said when Todd released him.

"Are you insane? We set off the alarm."

"We're wearing masks." Adam tugged at his, as if Todd was too stupid to see it.

"Which wouldn't have helped when the cops arrived." Todd ripped his off, and the cold air bit into his sweat-soaked face.

Adam shoved him. "Whose side are you on?"

For once, Todd shoved him back. "The side keeping you out of jail." There was that sensation again, the feeling that he was the older brother.

"Fuck you." Adam stomped off.

Todd growled and kicked a nearby box. A cat yowled. Great. Now I can add animal abuse to my record. Thinking of Fifi, Todd crouched and moved the box aside. A mangy cat hissed and darted away. Todd's kick couldn't have hurt it too much if it still had an attitude. What a night. The best he could say was he hadn't accidentally killed a cat.

Todd meandered through alleys, in no hurry to get home. The cold cut through his flimsy black attire, and he felt as if ice water flowed through his veins. His fingers numbed. He curled his full fingers into a fist to warm them. He wished he'd worn mittens, but even more, he longed for Claire's hands to warm his.

CHAPTER 16

When Todd woke, Adam had already left. Whether to school or somewhere else, Todd didn't know. Todd rolled over and checked the clock. He'd slept through his art class study session, which was fine because he'd slept through civics too. Unfortunately, he'd also missed economics.

His stomach growled. He'd woken in time to eat a late lunch and catch Claire after school for damage control. Todd forced himself to shower first. He couldn't face Claire smelling like a back alley. Once clean, he trotted downstairs, but he screeched to a halt in the kitchen.

A man sat at the counter wearing nothing but boxers. Todd's mom must not be catching the most civilized fish anymore, because the stranger munched with his mouth open, blotchy pink face shiny with sweat that dripped off his bulbous nose. Hope he's loaded.

Todd's mother forbade him from interacting with her boyfriends, but Todd was tired and cranky and hungry, so he trudged toward the fridge anyway. His heavy steps drew the man's attention. He stared at Todd, but Todd stared at the man's lunch.

The stranger filled his fork with the leftover Cajun sweet potatoes Claire had given Todd.

"This is great." He lifted the fork to his mouth and chomped.

Todd's blood pumped every muscle taut until he swelled to twice his size. His vision went red, and heat flushed his face.

He bit his tongue until it bled. He could beat this guy into the gray mush the school's cafeteria served, but rich men had power. Todd and

Adam had learned the hard way not to pick fights with their mother's boyfriends.

Todd strained his willpower to the max forcing himself to retreat into the basement. He beelined for his stash of Ides of March and rolled a joint. Within minutes, the high calmed his blood to a simmer.

The high was more intense than usual. Todd hadn't smoked in weeks. He'd been trying to stay alert in class and to smell nice for Claire. She wouldn't appreciate his smelling like pot when he explained away his absence, but at least he wouldn't have blood on his hands.

When he was confident he wouldn't pulverize his mother's latest benefactor, he returned to the kitchen. The man was gone. So were the leftovers. Todd wolfed down a PB&J and walked to school, not bothering with a jacket. He needed the cold to chill his lingering temper before he interacted with Claire.

Passing time provided the perfect cover for his entrance. He drifted through the crowd until he found Claire's locker. He waved, but she didn't wave back.

The fury in her green eyes pinned him still as her long legs carried her across the hallway. He saw her fist coming, but being high dampened his reaction time. Volleyball gave her wicked arm strength, so when her punch connected with his left eye, it knocked him flat.

"Fuck you, you shit-faced lying bastard."

Todd rubbed his eye, vaguely aware of the crowd that formed around them. "I—"

"They have ssssecurity cameras, dumbass."

Shit. She knew he'd vandalized the florist's shop. A teacher tried to reach them, but the circle of spectators thickened into a barricade.

"D-did you think I wouldn't find out? Do you think I'm ssss-stupid?"

"No, I—"

"Shut the fuck up." Claire shook her head. "All that talk about second chances. It was all bullshit, wasn't it?"

"No, Claire..." He tried to rise, but his head pounded. He was already losing part of his vision as his eye swelled.

Claire towered over him, and she over enunciated her next words. "Stay the hell away from me." She pushed through the crowd. The teacher tried to apprehend her, but she shook him off and marched straight to the principal's office.

She'd get detention, even though he'd committed the crime. He'd never heard her swear so much. He thought back to her comment that Saafi made her feel like a terrible person, but she wouldn't have uttered so much profanity if he hadn't betrayed her. Her friends were right. He was a bad influence.

Todd laid his head on the linoleum floor as the crowd dispersed. The bell rang, and the hallway descended into a blissful silence. Someone nudged his foot.

"You okay, son?" Principal Evans stood over him.

"I'm not your son." Todd struggled to his feet and started toward the door.

"Claire Peterson is in my office."

Todd halted.

"According to her file, you bring out the worst in her."

"They wrote that?"

"I read between the lines."

"Then give me detention instead of her." Todd reached for the door handle.

"I'm afraid I can't do that."

Todd whirled, one step shy of giving the principal his own black eye. "Why not?"

Principal Evans grinned with the satisfaction of a spider who'd caught a fly. Todd doubted the fly was Claire.

"As she confessed the moment she stepped into my office, she broke the school policies on fighting and using respectful language. Doesn't show a speck of regret, not that I blame her."

"That's not fair, I—"

"You need to learn that your actions have consequences for more than just you. If you care about Claire, man up and act like it." He strolled away, as if he'd just signed for a package instead of reprimanding a student for fighting.

Todd seethed his whole walk home, sick of everyone and everything: the principal's presumption, his mom's boyfriends, his brother's schemes, Maite's smugness, Claire's self-righteousness, his father's abandonment...his own failures.

He passed his house and stormed into the greenhouse, but the warm scent of plant life didn't calm him. This year, he'd studied harder than ever. He'd watched his language, and he'd even cut back on smoking, but everything he did to win Claire pulled him farther away from Adam. Now they were both pissed at him.

Todd screamed and shoved a planter, which hit the cement floor with a crash. Todd knelt in the spilled dirt, not caring that the broken pottery cut into his knees. The guidance counselor was right. He was a failure. He'd always been a failure, and he'd always be a failure.

Someone cleared their throat. Todd looked up to see Noah standing at the edge of the dirt pile. He handed Todd a broom.

"You make a mess. You clean it up."

Todd accepted the broom, grateful to be given a task instead of another lecture. Principal Evans's heart-to-heart had been one too many already. The plants had established roots, so he salvaged and repotted most of them. After a few broom strokes, the floor passed inspection. If only he could clean the rest of his life so easily.

Todd paused, broom still in hand. *"You make a mess. You clean it up."* Noah had been lecturing him. The guy had never mastered multiplication tables, but he understood life better than most teachers.

Todd raced to the front office, leaping over tool carts and hoses as he went.

"Noah?" He caught his breath. "Can I borrow your toolkit? I have another mess to clean."

* * *

Todd had hoped the bus ride to the florist would give him time to prepare himself to face Maite, but the trip only heightened his tension. A bulky, stubby-fingered teenager with a toolkit was an oddity by itself, but his black eye drew even more stares. When his stop arrived, he leaped off the bus as fast as the heavy toolbox allowed.

As predicted, the fearsome four were already there. Beth, Saafi, Maite, and Claire had pulled aside the temporary plastic barrier and were hauling debris to the alleyway dumpster. Adam's brick had knocked over several displays in addition to breaking the window.

The girls chatted as they worked, but the conversation ceased when they spotted Todd.

"What are you d-doing here?" Claire's breath puffed between her lips like smoke from a dragon's maw.

Todd held up Noah's toolkit. "I came to help."

The girls stared, not gesturing for him to join them. Todd considered turning around, but what would running home accomplish?

"Ah, Noah's stray returns to the crime scene."

Everyone turned to see Ms. Rojas passing into the main room.

Maite frowned. "Abuela, you need to sleep more."

Ms. Rojas, Maite's grandmother if Todd's sparse Spanish vocabulary could be trusted, waved away her concerns.

"Todd, join me in my office."

Todd followed her to an office whose door sported an opaque glass window reminiscent of old detective movies. Ms. Rojas clutched her sweater around herself and sat behind the desk.

"We are lucky it's not too cold today, or I'd worry about the plumbing bursting."

Todd hesitated before taking a seat. Maite loomed in the corner like a bodyguard. Todd restrained a grimace. She had good reason to think she needed to.

Maite's grandmother flipped her computer screen toward him and tapped a button. A black and white video played, the security footage showing Todd and Adam vandalizing the front window.

"If you want to get away with a crime, wear gloves."

Todd stared at his stubby fingers. He hadn't considered they might identify him. "I'll help you clean up, and I'm sure Noah will let you keep your flowers at his place. Er, where are the flowers?" Panic gripped him as he recalled the vacant store. Had they all frozen?

"We spent all night moving them into our apartment. Luckily for you, this building has a split thermostat." She eyed the video screen. "You have no problem painting vile words on my window, but you draw the line at breaking it?"

Todd didn't know how to respond. The line seemed clear to him. Spray paint was a prank that would create more work for Maite. Breaking windows was a crime that could ruin their business.

"Noah wouldn't let me set foot in his greenhouse if I slaughtered so many innocent plants."

Ms. Rojas chuckled. Maite scowled, but she kept quiet as her grandmother considered Todd.

"You're lucky my flowers survived. I'm doing a wedding tomorrow, and I wouldn't have time to ship replacements from my winter supplier. You would have cost me a lot of money, not to mention damaged the reputation I've spent twenty-eight years building."

Todd hung his head, thinking about what would happen to Noah and Mrs. Thompson if someone damaged the greenhouse.

"I'll tell you what. You clean the shop and transfer the inventory to Noah's, and I won't press charges."

"Abuela," Maite protested, but her grandmother held her hand out to Todd.

Todd shook it. "Deal."

They returned to the main room, and Todd helped the others clean. The girls shifted so that someone always stood between Todd and Saafi, who seemed oblivious to her protection detail.

"All right," Ms. Rojas said once they'd cleared the debris. "We're moving the flowers I don't need for the wedding to the Thompsons' greenhouse. Beth, if you're willing to drive too, we should only need one trip."

Beth nodded, and the group mounted the stairs to the small apartment on the second floor. The others trudged inside, but Todd stood in the doorway in stunned wonder. He had never smelled such potent perfume. The greenhouse smelled nice, but their plants didn't bloom simultaneously. Todd's eyes watered as he took in the colorful flowers packed into the living room. Ms. Rojas had channeled nature into an artistic masterpiece more magnificent than anything Oliver had shown the class.

Todd shook himself before the girls noticed him stalling. He picked up a box filled with pre-made bouquets and hauled it downstairs. Beth followed him.

"You'd better not give my sister any of that Tides of March crap you smoke."

"Ides of March."

Beth caught his eye over the box she carried. "I wouldn't have thought potheads were history buffs."

Todd held the door open for her with his foot. "The grower calls himself Caesar. He's a little batty. Made me rethink my habits."

"Your BO says otherwise." Beth wrinkled her nose as she led him to her car, where she opened the trunk and deposited the flowers. "Just stay away from Minh."

Her face filled with an emotion Todd couldn't identify because it wasn't the anger he usually received. Anxiety? He'd thought Beth hated him like everyone else, but what if she just worried about her sister?

An overprotective sibling, he understood. Todd tilted his head, as if viewing her from a different angle would help him distinguish contempt from concern.

"Minh hasn't asked me for anything. I don't think you need to worry about her caving to peer pressure. She's pretty headstrong."

"You're telling me." Beth's look of concern deepened. "She's growing up, and she's cute. I don't like the guys she attracts. The last idiot to skulk outside her window had so many piercings sticking out of his face he looked like an overgrown porcupine."

Todd chuckled. He could see Minh attracting that type. "I think she'll be fine. I'm arguably the worst influence in school, and spending art class with me hasn't corrupted her."

"Huh." Beth looked simultaneously relieved and stressed, as if she'd forgotten Todd was worse than Porcupine Face. "I guess better you than Adam." She marched back into the store for more flowers.

Todd followed her, unsure what to think of his elevation from "bath drain scum" to "better than Adam." His brother always bested him at socializing, but maybe Todd had been competing in the wrong arena. Would he have an edge in the decent-human-being circle?

They finished loading the cars, and Ms. Rojas, Beth, and Saafi drove to Noah's. Maite looked conflicted about staying behind, but she must have deemed Todd a threat needing supervision. Too bad. He would have liked time alone with Claire, not that she'd spoken over two words to him.

Todd helped Maite heft a piece of plywood over the gap where the window had been, and Claire fixed it into place. When they finished, Maite sank to the floor. Todd hadn't noticed the bags beneath her eyes before. Sitting there, she didn't look like the monstrous bodyguard he feared. She looked tired and...hurt.

"Why d-did you do it?" Claire asked as she sat beside Maite.

Todd sat cross-legged in front of them. "Adam is my brother."

"Okay, why did Adam do it?"

"Maite called the cops on him."

"What?" Maite straightened.

"You didn't?" Todd said.

"No." Maite's eyes darkened. "But I will if I catch him with drugs in my neighborhood."

"Huh." Todd glanced toward the boarded-up window. All that damage, for no reason. He was glad to know the truth, but he wouldn't tell Adam. His brother would hunt down the real tattletales, and who knew what revenge he'd seek when he found them?

"Why do you fight?" Maite asked.

"What do you mean?"

"I fight to protect people smaller than me: Abuela, Saafi, Betty, Clara..." She nudged Claire with a grin that suggested Claire could take care of herself. "Why do you fight?" She gestured to the broken window.

Todd picked up a plastic label they'd missed while sweeping and fidgeted with it. "I told you. Adam is my brother."

"And he's worth fffffighting for?" Claire asked.

Todd met her eye. "He's my brother." Beth might understand, but neither of them would. They didn't have siblings.

Then again, they understood the loyalty owed a friend. Was it so different? He'd always thought of Maite as a bully, but his encounters

108

with her suggested she only used her fists when someone else threatened her loved ones. Apparently, making out with Claire counted as a threat. Todd had vandalized her grandmother's shop because he'd thought she'd threatened Adam. Were they just two loyal people needlessly fighting on opposite sides?

Todd had labeled these girls the fearsome four, but the more he saw, the more he reconsidered his first impressions. Saafi wasn't the snooty know-it-all he'd pegged her as last year. She had a tender heart and forgave too quickly. Beth's sharp wit arose from her selfless concern for her sister. Maite worked as hard for her grandmother as Todd did for Noah, and Claire... Claire wasn't just fun at parties. She'd overcome her grief and fought for the future she wanted.

Adam considered the girls enemies, but were they? Did they need to fight?

The door opened, and Saafi entered, nose in her phone.

"We're ordering pizza. Ms. Rojas voted for Hawaiian. Any other suggestions?"

"I'll pay." Todd rose, triggering Maite to spring up after him. The girls stared, as if waiting for him to shout "psych" and break something. He gestured to the boarded-up window. "I'm guessing pizza costs less than glass."

"If Todd is buying," Ms. Rojas said, "let's add an order of breadsticks."

"Hawaiian pizza with breadsticks. Thanks for dinner, Todd." Saafi exchanged a knowing grin with Ms. Rojas, and Todd couldn't help wondering why the people he'd hurt the most forgave him first.

Chapter 17

Todd's backpack clunked as he swung it over his shoulder. He'd been carrying Claire's washed-out leftover containers, waiting for a day when Adam ditched school. He hadn't waited long. His brother's school attendance was getting shoddy, so much so that Todd started walking to school so his brother could drive in late if needed.

Tardiness wasn't the only change in Adam. He stayed out later, even on school nights. When he was home, he paced and muttered to himself. People wouldn't need to check their hands to tell them apart anymore. Adam had lost weight, making Todd the more muscular twin.

Todd felt like he was struggling up a hill that his brother was sliding down. He didn't know how to help either of them, but Claire had her life together, even after last year's drama, even after losing both parents. She'd solidified her dreams into goals. If anyone could anchor him to decency, she could.

Todd skipped the cafeteria line, knowing he had only a few precious moments to catch Claire alone. Sure enough, she sat by herself, eating her packed lunch while her friends stood in line. Before he could second-guess himself, he set the clean containers on the table between them.

Claire eyed the bowls and lids. "They're d-disposable."

"I know. I wanted an excuse to talk to you outside of econ." After witnessing his mom's boyfriend polish off the leftovers, he'd contemplated trashing, crushing, or even burning the dishes. He was glad he hadn't. "I have an idea for researching our project."

"You couldn't have told me in class?"

"We had a test today, remember?" One he'd passed thanks to Cathryn's help, but the exam was a convenient excuse. He'd wanted to talk to Claire without her friends eavesdropping. She'd be more likely to agree to his plan without the positive peer pressure. A manipulative strategy, he admitted, but he'd worry about morality later.

Claire stacked the containers and pushed them into her backpack. "I'm listening."

"I think we should visit this restaurant." Told handed her the menu he'd printed from the website. "They only serve vegetarian food, but it's a farm-to-table place with a seasonal menu like you want. I already called the owners, and they said they'd be happy to give us an inside look into the business."

"That's...a really good idea." Her tone suggested she hated admitting it.

"Great. Meet me at the front entrance after school." Todd took off before her friends arrived, leaving her no time to object.

The afternoon passed with agonizing slowness. He tried to remember Cathryn's acronyms in civics, but his nerves jumbled the letters. When the last bell rang, he cantered to the front entrance, unable to restrain himself to a casual walk. Claire arrived a moment later, green eyes fierce.

"If you think I'm getting in a c-c-car with you, you're wrong."

Todd grinned. "We're taking the bus." He strode toward the street, hoping she'd follow.

"You're lucky I don't have practice tonight," Claire said after catching up with him

I'll take all the luck I can get. The bus arrived. Todd plunked his change into the receptacle while Claire tapped her pass on the reader. She frowned when he sat beside her, but she didn't ask him to move, which Todd took as a win.

The bus transported them to the invisible boundary between city and suburb. The restaurant, Green Thumb, nestled on the corner like a houseplant. Even from the street, they saw the green décor through the wooden windows.

Todd opened the door for Claire, assuming that's what gentlemen did. The smell combined the greenhouse and Midtown Global Market. His stomach reminded him it had been a long time since he'd eaten more than frozen pizza and the school's gray mush.

"Welcome to Green Thumb. Table for two?" The tiny woman spoke so quickly Todd's ears suffered whiplash. Adding to her childlike appearance, she wore her short black hair in pigtails, and her tawny-gold face was clear of makeup.

"Actually, we're here to see Gabriela Foreman."

"You must be Todd!" The woman broke into a huge smile as she shook their hands. "I'm Gabby. I run the place." Her gesture encompassed the entire restaurant. "Come on, I'll show you around."

Her pigtails bounced as she bounded away. Todd and Claire struggled to keep up.

"I'm g-guessing you serve coffee here too?" Claire asked.

"What was your first clue?" Gabby's laugh had a manic tint to it. "I can live without meat, but caffeine and I are like this." She crossed her fingers.

Gabby swept them into an office that had nothing childish about it. A large filing cabinet dominated one corner, and papers lay organized with military precision in trays labeled DUE and PAID.

"This is where I keep track of everything: inventory orders, utility bills, customer feedback, you name it."

Claire whipped out her phone, fingers flying as she typed notes. Todd wondered how she kept up with the caffeinated woman.

"How do you sssss-sssstock fresh vegetables in the winter?" she asked.

"George's family owns an organic farm in Oklahoma. They send us a truckload once a week. Oh, I should introduce you to George." She led them through a back door to an industrial kitchen. Claire's eyes sparkled as she admired the fixtures.

"My husband, George." Gabby gestured to a man who manned the stove like a conductor before an orchestra. His deep brown skin glistened with sweat. "I handle the business side, and he cooks. George!" She leaned close to Todd and whispered, "He has a bad ear, but he's too stubborn to wear his hearing aid." She shouted again, "These are the kids with the economics project."

George saluted them with a spatula and returned to cooking.

"He's not related to George Foreman," Gabby said.

"Who?" Todd asked.

For the first time since they met, Gabby stood still. "I'm getting old." Her bounce returned. "I'll clear you a table and have George fix you dinner. On the house!" She charged out of the kitchen, deposited them at an open table, and zipped off to greet another couple who'd just arrived.

Todd and Claire sat in silence, letting their senses calm down after the Gabby overload, but Gabby soon returned with two steaming plates.

"We make all our pasta fresh in house," she said as she set the dishes on the table. She buzzed away before they could thank her.

Todd took a bite of the roasted vegetables and savored the rich tomato sauce. "Mmmm. Not that I'm turning vegetarian, but this is amazing."

Claire nodded. "It might be sssssss-ssssss-wise to add some vegetarian dishes to our menu."

As they ate, Todd surveyed the restaurant's interior. Potted plants stood in every corner, and several hung from the ceiling in baskets. He liked how the décor made the place feel alive. Even the paintings featured plants. The one beside their table depicted a farm—George's?

"Do you ever miss living on a farm?" Todd asked.

Claire slowed her chewing. "It's c-complicated."

Todd waited for her to continue. She squirmed before acquiescing.

"It's hard to make friends in a small t-town when you're d-different."

"It's not exactly easy here," Todd muttered.

"It is if you're not a jerk."

Todd stuffed food into his mouth to avoid responding to that. Claire took another bite, and he thought their conversation was over, but she surprised him by speaking again.

"I mmmiss getting fresh produce for cheap, and there was no traffic or ssssmog. The farm was quiet. Peaceful."

"That sounds nice."

Claire pushed her food around her plate. "Maybe it's easier as an adult."

Todd thought of his parents, thought of how some customers treated Noah. "Adults can be jerks too."

"Yeah, I guess so."

Todd finished his last bite. "It doesn't matter where you live. Find the people worth loving and forget everyone else."

"Yeah. You're right." Claire eyed him as if wondering which category he belonged in.

His hope parasite took root inside him again as he willed her to pick the former.

CHAPTER 18

Todd scratched his head at Cathryn's civics lesson. "I still don't get why Iowa goes first."

"They have a long nominating process, so they start early." Cathryn shrugged. "Not everything in politics makes sense."

"Most of it doesn't," Minh said. She was using paper pieces to form her art today. Todd hadn't paid attention when Oliver had explained the process. Civics and economics worried him more than art.

"How was your not-date with Claire?" Minh asked as she glued paper pieces to the poster board backing.

"Do you always spy on your sister's friends?" Todd asked.

"Of course. Now answer the question."

Todd chuckled, thinking the overprotective sibling mentality went both ways. "She hasn't decided whether she still hates me."

"It's amazing she allows you within a twenty-mile radius after what you did," Minh said, obviously in the know about Todd's vandalism escapade.

"I'm trying to do better."

"You got a funny way of showing it," Minh said. "Hand me that calligraphy pen, will you?"

"Minh has a point," Cathryn said as she handed Minh the pen and a bottle of ink. "People often say they'll change. Few do." Her face fell, and Todd wondered whether she spoke from experience.

Minh dipped the pen in the ink. "If you've changed, prove it."

Cathryn nodded. "'Well done is better than well said.'"

"More Benjamin Franklin quotes?" Todd said, not in the mood for a history lesson.

"If it's true, it doesn't matter who said it." Minh added some artful words over her paper-piecing. "You need to show Claire you're a good guy now."

"I took her to a restaurant," Todd said.

"It doesn't count if it's just the two of you. Lots of guys perform for a pretty face, but they become scum when the girl isn't looking."

Cathryn nodded. "A true inward change manifests in outward, public behavior."

Todd raked his fingers through his hair, wondering again why girls were so complicated. "Okay, so how do I prove myself?"

Minh held up her finished creation. Colored paper pieces swirled in the background, and the word MOSAIC stood out in the middle. Mosaic, aka Saafi's multicultural student group, the one she formed after Todd and Adam put that WHITES ONLY sign on the drinking fountain.

"No. No way."

Minh lowered her art. "So much for pursuing decency."

"Avoiding people I pissed off last year doesn't make me a bad person."

"But it does make you a coward."

Coward. That word always punched him in the gut.

"Attending the group would reverse your public statement of allegiance," Cathryn said.

"Let me translate that from genius-speak," Minh said. "You hurt a lot of people last year. If you want to undo some of the damage, risk getting hurt yourself."

Cathryn furrowed her brow. "That's not what I meant."

Minh dismissed her with a wave. "Your fancy gift baskets won't mean squat if you keep your butt safely on the sidelines."

Oliver interrupted to evaluate "their" work, expressing disapproval for Minh's "commercializing art," but the bell rang before he could criticize her overmuch. Todd hurried out of class lest the girls continue badgering him.

After Mr. Patel's lecture, Claire dove right into her new ideas for their project. Their restaurant trip must have inspired her because she chatted at light speed, stuttering with abandon. Did that mean she felt at ease with him? Comfortable enough not to monitor her speech and use strategies to diminish her stutter?

He listened without responding, basking in her happiness more than attending to her words, but it was a hollow victory, and he knew it. Minh was right. Winning Claire's trust required sacrifice, not bribery.

Mastering his nerves had allowed Todd to become one of the state's best football kickers, but none of his tried-and-true strategies worked. All afternoon, he shook with a cold sweat. No one considered school lunch gourmet, but Todd couldn't stomach even one bite. After the final bell, he dragged his feet to the classroom where the group met, but he had to pause when vertigo overwhelmed him.

He forced himself to enter the classroom, but when everyone inside stared at him, his vocal cords malfunctioned. This was a mistake. His instincts impelled him to flee, but his legs stiffened into planks. Maite stood, but to Todd's surprise, someone else spoke first.

"What are you doing here?" Jeff Chen, whom Todd had once considered a friend, hurled the question at him like a mace.

"Am I—" Todd cleared his throat, embarrassed by the nervous squeak that had emerged. "Am I not allowed?"

"That depends." Saafi, who led the circle of students, spoke with a diplomat's calm. "Are you here to cause trouble or to learn?"

"Uh, learn."

"Then welcome." She gestured to a chair in the circle, but Todd felt the collective heat of twenty angry glares. Only their respect for Saafi prevented them from mauling Todd on the spot.

He sank into a chair outside the circle, out of range of Maite's fists. Saafi pursed her lips as if debating whether to push the issue, but she must have decided to accept baby steps.

"We were discussing different family structures. For example, I live with my dad, aunt, and four cousins."

Todd glanced around the room, but the angry faces didn't hint at the expected response.

"Who do you live with?" Saafi asked, like a preschool teacher coaxing a shy toddler into class.

"Oh. It's just Mom, Adam, and me." Adam's name sent a ripple of whispers around the circle, like an angrier game of telephone, but Saafi redirected the conversation.

Each person shared their family life. Claire had grown up on her grandparents' farm and now lived with her aunt. Maite joined her grandmother in America after her parents died, and Beth lived with her parents and a gaggle of adopted siblings. Jeff Chen lived with his aunt and uncle. Why hadn't Todd known that? Hadn't they been friends?

Todd was already the odd one out, but as the conversation shifted to family norms, the differences between him and his classmates intensified. As Todd guessed, Claire's aunt expected her to keep the apartment spotless. Beth couldn't interrupt her parents' church group "unless I'm bleeding or the house is on fire." Maite prayed the rosary with her grandmother every morning. Jeff's aunt and uncle insisted he fill up the gas tank after he borrowed the car.

The students in the group represented a variety of cultures, but their families all set expectations at home. Todd's mother had one rule: stay out of the way. As Todd listened to the others complain, he couldn't help feeling envious. Their families cared whether they came home at night. Todd wondered whether his father set rules for his other kids, whether he cared enough to ensure they grew into decent human beings.

Todd had planned to dart out the door as soon as the group ended, but his contemplation stole his focus, and he missed his chance. He'd have to wait until everyone left if he wanted to avoid potential confrontations. Most people departed, but some gathered protectively around Saafi as she approached him.

"I'm glad you came, Todd. Why don't you bring something to share next week?"

"What?" Todd hadn't realized he was signing himself up for show and tell.

"Yeah, something from your home culture. For example, Claire brought cheese curds."

"Uh, I don't think—"

"You should invite Adam too."

A collective gasp sucked the oxygen from the room, but Saafi's serene smile settled her bodyguards. Todd wondered what it would be like to command such respect that a half-dozen belligerent students fell silent simply because you smiled.

"I don't think he'd be interested." The words scraped Todd's throat like jagged rocks.

Another collective gasp sounded as Saafi patted his arm. "Well, this is a good start."

She departed with her entourage, who appeared to wish this were the ending rather than the beginning.

Claire lingered. "Why did you c-ome?"

Todd tried to shrug, but he was so exhausted his shoulder merely twitched. "Something about an outward manifestation of an internal change."

"Oh. You came be-because someone told you to."

"I came because I want to win you back." Todd winced. He hadn't planned to reveal his true intentions to Claire until he was firmly back in her good graces.

Claire crossed her arms over her chest. "We never officially dated."

"We made out more than once." *Shit.* He'd spoken without thinking. Claire's face twisted in disgust.

"If you just want to mmmmmake out—"

"I don't want to make out." At Claire's questioning look, Todd palmed his neck. "I mean, I wouldn't *mind*, but I really want—" His mouth filled with cotton. "Never mind." He'd already botched this conversation, and he couldn't handle more. He was weak from not eating, sick from nerves, and embarrassed to admit the former two.

Todd hefted his backpack over his shoulder, but Claire blocked his path to the door.

"What do you want?" She spoke slowly, slurring smoothness into words she might otherwise stutter. "If it involves me, I have a right to know."

Todd glanced toward the window, but he'd probably break his ankle if he jumped from the second story. Claire was too tall and muscular to sneak past. His options were a) push her over or b) tell the truth. Neither was likely to get him a date.

Todd closed his eyes, too tired to play these games anymore. Girls were too complicated, and being a decent human being proved more stressful than he'd imagined. He may as well be honest.

"I just want to hold hands at the grocery store."

An involuntary giggle escaped Claire, but she covered it with a hand. "You want to hold hands at the grocery store?"

"Yeah. I mean, you know those old people who putter through the aisles? It's like, grocery shopping is their big event, and they just want to enjoy going out together." Todd rushed through his confession, hoping Claire's ridicule would be just as brief, but Claire didn't laugh. Her eyes twinkled, and her round face radiated a warmth he'd never seen from her.

"Well, then I G-uess I agree with Saafi. You're off to a good start." She winked and spun out the door.

Like an athlete who'd pushed himself beyond his limit, Todd experienced the sudden euphoria of a runner's high. I'm off to a good start. He practically skipped home, but he bounded straight into an argument.

"Don't get lippy with me," his mother said. She stood on a stool, wobbling on her high heels.

"I've been late a couple days. What's the big deal?" Adam said.

His mom cursed as her fingers missed whatever she sought. Todd tried to sneak past, but she caught him.

"Grab the margarita machine for me." Her tight dress hampered her movements as she hopped to the floor.

Adam gave him a sympathetic look as Todd scrambled up the stool and hunted through piles of kitchen stuff he hadn't known they owned. He pushed the clutter aside, revealing the MARGARITA MARTHA label. After tucking the cord around the machine, he dragged it out of the cupboard, but it was heavier than it appeared. Todd lost his grip, and it hit the floor with a crash.

"You useless fucking idiot." His mother yanked the stool out from under him, and he tumbled to the floor, bruising his elbow.

"Hey!" Adam moved between them.

"Don't 'hey' me. Your principal called during my lunch date." She seemed more irritated by the call's timing than its content. "I was planning to make up for the interruption with margaritas, but thanks to your butterfingered brother, that's no longer an option."

"I'm sure you have other methods of 'making up' with your boyfriends, Mom," Adam said.

"You're grounded."

"Oh, that's rich." Adam stepped toward her, highlighting the height difference that had inhibited their mother's discipline for years.

Todd scrambled to his feet, hoping his bulk would grant him the power to referee.

"Adam, it's not worth it." He nodded toward the stairs. *Don't provoke her.*

Their mother pointed. "You're. Grounded." She gave both syllables in "grounded" equal emphasis.

Adam's arm twitched, but Todd grabbed it and hauled him to their room. He collapsed into bed, but Adam paced.

"Why do we even listen to her anymore?"

"Because she can take away our car keys." And some day Claire might trust me to drive her to a real date. Not that he minded the bus, but cars were more...versatile.

Adam didn't appear to have heard him. His pacing grew more frantic. "I'm not taking shit from her anymore, from anyone."

"Yeah," Todd said, not sure how his statement differed from their usual approach to humanity.

Adam halted. "Where were you today, anyway? I checked your usual haunts."

Todd had avoided his favorite smoking hangouts so he'd smell better. Apparently, Claire preferred how he smelled after a day of nervous cold sweats to a day of relaxing smoking. Girls were vicious.

"Where have you been?" Todd said, unwilling to reveal he'd gone to the student group Adam tried to sabotage.

Adam's pacing resumed. "Doing damage control."

Todd leaned into his pillow. He'd worked hard to undo his brother's damage control, and he wasn't in the mood for more.

"Joey said the provider would only agree to a test deal." Adam spat into the dead marigold's pot, as if he couldn't understand why no one trusted him. "You need to convince Mrs. Thompson to let you start some Ides of March in the greenhouse. We'll need a bigger crop next year."

"For what?" Todd didn't point out that Noah managed the greenhouse now. Mixing Noah with Caesar struck him as a terrible idea.

Adam gestured to their room. "You want to live under her roof forever?"

"Ignore her, Adam."

"No." Adam's eyes darkened. "We can do better than this. We will do better than this." His tone reverberated with frustration. He might envision himself a drug lord with the entire city kissing his feet, but now he couldn't even peddle for a small-time dealer.

Todd just wanted to hold hands with a girl, but maybe romantic strolls through the grocery store were beyond his reach. Claire and her friends had families who supported them. Todd had a promiscuous mother, an absentee father, and a wannabe drug dealer brother. Even if he wanted to attend the next Mosaic meeting, what would he bring?

I'll never fit in.

CHAPTER 19

T odd reached the last bell without a hint of desire for a smoke. He'd arrived on time to his classes, aced his math test, and contributed to the economics project. Not that Mr. Patel acknowledged how well he and Claire were doing. He seemed to hold a grudge against them, but that only improved Todd's situation. Claire allied with him against the snooty teacher, and she enjoyed Todd's impression of him.

Todd strolled to his locker, looking forward to an afternoon in the greenhouse. He'd recycled some old socks into a chew toy for Fifi, and he couldn't wait to play with her. The dog enjoyed people, and the lonely winter months depressed her.

Adam was waiting for him, leaning against his locker. When he spotted Todd, he straightened.

"What the hell, man?"

"What?"

"I don't need to sleep with the Gossip Girls to learn you went to that group."

Todd's stomach turned to lead. "I was—"

"What, Todd?" Adam stepped inches from his face. "Fraternizing with the enemy? What's next, selling flowers with Maite?"

"No." Todd backed away. "It was nothing. I was just—"

"What?" Adam's voice was harsh, but soon realization dawned, and he rolled his eyes. "You were trying to get in Claire's pants. God, Todd. How long before you get over your redhead fetish?"

Todd restrained a frustrated growl. Better Adam think him horny than traitorous.

"As long as it takes to get laid," he muttered.

"Oh?" someone behind him said.

Todd and Adam whirled to see Claire charging through the hallway.

"Guess I don't have to t-t-tell you we're changing rooms."

"Stay away from my brother, you tongue-tied giraffe," Adam said.

"With pleasure." Claire stormed off.

"Claire—"

Adam grabbed him before he could follow her. "Let her go, man. I'll find you a sexier redhead." He tugged Todd toward the door. "I'll give you the details on the way home."

"Details?"

Adam paused. "The deal for Sunday night? The test? We need it to go perfectly."

"I don't—"

"Relax. I'll do the talking. You just loom menacingly."

Todd tore free of his brother's grip, but the gesture emphasized their widening size difference. Adam was rapidly losing weight while Todd gained muscle. If Adam completed this stupid deal, he'd need someone big along to defend him. Todd raised his eyes to the ceiling. Why is life so complicated?

"All right, where are we going?"

* * *

Todd glanced at Cathryn's window, but her whole house was dark. She and her family must be asleep.

"I thought Caesar banned us from dealing here."

"This is our home turf," Adam said, "and it's the least monitored option. Besides, we're not technically on Caesar's property."

Adam had chosen to meet in the burned ruins between Caesar's house and Cathryn's, perhaps to intimidate their contact. They had parked around the back of Caesar's place, out of sight in case they needed a quick getaway. They'd surveyed the perimeter after arriving. No surprises this time. Todd hoped there weren't any in their future. In taking the trouble farther away from Caesar, they'd brought it closer to Cathryn. He tried not to dwell on how much her tutoring had helped him. This deal better go smoothly.

Adam paced, his body twitching with more than his usual fidgeting. The nervous energy made Todd want to catch him and hold him still.

"Are you on something?" Todd asked. I thought you wanted to deal, not use.

Adam waved away his concern and continued pacing. "Just something to keep me alert."

Great. Before Todd could ask what Adam had taken, the sound of wheels grinding into the gravel reached them, and a pair of headlights lit the cul-de-sac. Adam and Todd stepped forward, but the car passed them and parked haphazardly in front of Cathryn's house. A large man emerged, mumbling to himself as he stumbled up the porch steps.

Adam checked his watch. "They'll be here in five minutes. We can't have that drunk bumbling around."

The man—Cathryn's father if the shadows weren't deceiving Todd's eyes—cursed as he dropped his keys. Instead of picking them up, he pounded the door and shouted.

"Bea! Let me in."

"Take care of him." Adam nudged Todd toward the house.

"What? What am I supposed to do?"

"I don't know. Knock him out or something." Adam shoved harder, pushing Todd a step forward. Todd crept along the gravel road, but when the man scanned his surroundings, he had to duck behind the car. He crouched beside the driver's-side door while the man hollered.

"Bea! Open up." He pounded once for every syllable.

Another pair of headlights came into view, but the man continued pounding. Todd looked at his hands. He'd battled in his fair share of fist fights, but sneaking up behind a drunk seemed wrong.

Their contact's car parked near the ruins. Todd glanced at the man. He had to do something. Now.

Todd braced himself and stood, but the house's door opened. He ducked back behind the car and peered over the hood as Cathryn's face filled the doorway.

"Where's your mother?" the man slurred. Todd couldn't hear Cathryn's reply, but he saw the man push her aside as he entered the house. Cathryn's shoulder hit the doorframe, and she rubbed it as she retrieved the man's fallen keys. She lifted her eyes, and Todd flattened his back to the car. Could she see him? He held his breath until he heard the door close, then crept through the shadows to his brother.

Todd tried to calm his racing heart as Adam talked. His panting wouldn't intimidate anyone. After agonizing minutes, money changed hands, and the contact drove off. Todd's knees threatened to buckle, but at least they'd finished the deal.

Adam handed Todd half the cash. "See? Told you we'd do better." He clapped Todd on the shoulder and strode to their waiting car.

Todd looked up at the second story of Cathryn's house. Light glowed from the window, and Cathryn was staring at him.

CHAPTER 20

Adam threw a pillow at his alarm, but Todd forced himself to heed the early wake-up call. He wanted to get to art early.

As expected, Cathryn had also arrived early, though she didn't appear as exhausted as he was. Maybe the makeup covered her sleep deprivation.

Todd plopped his backpack beside her. "So, your dad—"

"Is none of your business," Cathryn said, fixing her gaze on the flashcards she was making. "And even if it were, can a drug dealer judge an alcoholic?"

Todd's protest died in his throat. When he peddled the Ides of March, he considered it a favor to his fellow potheads, but last night, his title changed to drug dealer.

Todd stared at the table, ceding the moral ground but not quite ready to relinquish his concern for Cathryn.

"Minh doesn't know, does she?"

"Would you tell your friends?"

Todd grimaced. Once again, she had him. He never spoke about his mother's exploits.

"I can take care of myself, Todd," Cathryn said. "If you want to help, stop bringing trouble to my house."

Given his firsthand witness of how well she lied, Todd wasn't sure he believed her, but Oliver strode into the room before he could question her further. Minh rolled in as the teacher described the prompt. She grabbed a few hunks of charcoal before joining their table.

Cathryn held up a civics flashcard. "A flip-flop is a derogatory term for a sudden change of opinion by a public official. It is an ugly form of hypocrisy, like saying you're going to respect someone's privacy and then showing up at their doorstep."

Cathryn spoke in her usual academic tone, but her meaning was clear. Todd vowed to force Adam to deal somewhere else. He couldn't sober up Cathryn's father, but he could at least protect her from further trouble.

"Or," Minh added, "like faking interest in a student group when you just want to bang a redhead."

How did she hear about that? Todd glared at her, but she didn't look up from her drawing.

"You're nosy, you know that?"

"That's what little sisters are for." Minh's fingers grew black as she added some dark shading along the edge of her paper.

Glad I have a brother. "If you're going to meddle, be helpful. How do I get back into Claire's goodwill? Another apology basket?"

"Decent human beings stick to their principles." Minh squinched up her face as if her nose itched, but she didn't want to scratch it with charcoal-dusted fingers.

"No flip-flopping," Cathryn said. "If you say you'll do something, do it."

"I need to go to Mosaic again?"

"You need to pick a side." Minh gave up and rubbed her nose, leaving a small smudge.

"I'm not ditching my brother."

"Your brother obviously doesn't want you to date Claire," Cathryn said. "You can't please them both. There's a reason voters despise flip-flopping politicians."

Todd considered that as they finished their study session. She's wrong. He could date Claire without betraying Adam. He'd just have to separate them. Adam's poor attendance should facilitate that.

The art teacher hopped over to their table—literally. Yesterday, he'd lectured them at length about transcending generic modes of locomotion. Before he even asked, Minh held up her charcoal drawing. The portrait split down the middle, with Todd's and Adam's faces each forming half. Todd appeared confused, as Minh had likely seen him while he was studying with Cathryn. Adam's eyes held a dangerous gleam, and his half of their smile had an uncomfortable edge reminiscent of horror movie clowns.

"I love how you captured the difference between the two twins," Oliver said.

"Oh, that isn't Adam," Minh said. "Those are both Todd." She slid the page to Todd as the bell rang.

The class filed out, which didn't prevent Oliver from gushing over Minh's "brave statement about the dualities within us all." Todd stared at the charcoal drawing that may as well be an x-ray of his soul. Was she right? Were these the two paths Principal Evans said he was straddling?

No. He could be a decent human being and a loyal brother. He just had to work harder.

Todd dumped the picture into the trash, but Minh and Cathryn were still waiting for the elevator outside the classroom. He averted his eyes, but someone else had already captured their attention.

"You have dirt on your face." Big Brody loomed in the stairwell, grinning at the charcoal smudge on Minh's nose.

Minh shifted forward in her chair. "Yet I'm still more attractive than you."

"Minh," Cathryn whispered.

"At least my legs work." Brody stepped out of the shadows, and Cathryn shrank into the corner. "Can you even have sex?"

"Yes," Minh said, holding her ground, "but I'm not into pig-gorilla hybrids."

"You little bitch on wheels." Brody drew his fist back like an archer drawing a bow, but Todd lunged for him. He grabbed Brody's arm and pulled him off balance.

"Get off me." Brody shook loose of Todd's grip.

"They're sophomore girls, Brody. Leave them alone."

Brody's lips twisted into a sneer, revealing bits of his morning cupcake between his teeth.

"I thought you were on our side."

"I'm not on the side that picks on people half their size." Less than that. Minh and Cathryn combined wouldn't come close to Brody's weight.

Brody shook his head, but instead of responding, he punched Todd in the gut. Todd doubled over, and Brody shoved him across the hall. He hit the ground with a thud. Todd scrambled to his feet as Brody lunged for Minh, but Minh sprayed something, and the big guy screamed and scratched at his eyes.

"Bitch on wheels?" Minh grinned. "I like that. I'll have to put it on a bumper sticker."

"You pepper sprayed him?" Todd joined her in watching Brody writhe on the floor.

"No. I used a less irritating pepper spray alternative because I'm not allowed to carry real pepper spray until I'm sixteen, and I can't get a stun gun until I'm eighteen." Minh's tone suggested she considered the prohibition as ridiculous as the law prohibiting crossing the Wisconsin border with a duck on your head. "If you'd stayed out of the fight, I'd have spared you a bruised rib."

Todd grimaced as he probed his injury. He'd sport an ugly bruise.

"What happened?" The group turned as Principal Evans descended the stairs.

Oliver poked his head out of the classroom. "These students are corrupting the artistic environment with their negative vibes."

Principal Evans gaped, as if wondering why the art teacher summoned him to the bowels of the school over negative vibes, but then he spotted Brody. The big teen curled himself into the fetal position, and Principal Evans targeted his gaze at Todd.

"I didn't—he—it wasn't my fault," Todd said.

"Todd is right." Cathryn extracted herself from the corner and stood beside Minh. "Brody was the aggressor. Todd was just trying to help."

Principal Evans shifted his gaze from Todd to Brody and back. "When I said you should better yourself, this wasn't what I meant."

"I just took a punch. She's the one who pepper sprayed him." Todd pointed at Minh.

"Wow, Todd. Way to pass the blame to the damsel in distress."

Todd snorted. "You don't look distressed to me."

"Enough," Principal Evans said. "Minh, pepper spray is prohibited on school grounds."

"Pepper spray *alternative*. I didn't think Oliver would appreciate it if I set off my alarm and strobe light. Half the girls in school started carrying self-defense key chains after last year." She glared at Todd as if to say, "This doesn't redeem you." Todd grimaced, but she returned her attention to the principal. "My dad filled out a ton of paperwork on the subject. I'm sure you'll find it in Principal Gray's records."

"Principal Gray wasn't the most organized with his paperwork." Principal Evans's tone suggested his predecessor wasn't that organized about anything. "I'll look into it. In the meantime, you three get to class. I'll help Brody to the nurse's office."

"And keep your negative vibes away from my creative space." Oliver shooed them. Todd could have sworn Principal Evans rolled his eyes as he hefted Brody to his feet.

Todd hustled through the halls, but by the time he reached economics, class was ending.

"I'm sorry I'm late, I—"

"Save it," Claire said as she packed her things.

"Claire, I—"

"I don't want to hear your lllllies." She joined her friends. Saafi gave him a disappointed head shake before she followed Claire out of the room.

The one time Todd had made the honorable choice, and Claire wouldn't believe him. His bad luck plagued his whole day. Adam was who knew where at lunch, so he choked down the gray mush alone. He failed a pop quiz in civics, and the Gossip Girls wouldn't stop pointing at him as they whispered.

Principal Evans never summoned him to the office, so he assumed he hadn't earned detention for his role in the pepper spray incident. When the last bell rang, Todd headed straight for the old wing. Forget the smell. He needed a smoke.

The usual stoners cast shifty glances at him. Perhaps they'd already heard the report from the Gossip Girls. Not wanting to explain the rumors, Todd exited the building and headed to his other favorite smoke spot—a warm place by the brick wall.

Someone grabbed his jacket hood and yanked him back.

"That was a test." Big Brody shoved him against the wall. His eyes were still bloodshot. "You failed."

"What?" Even if Todd had been able to wiggle free, two guys he didn't recognize appeared at Brody's side. One of them had a large nose ring, like a bull.

"Adam said we could trust you," Bull Guy's companion said. His red sweatshirt was stained with something blue, like spilled sports drink.

"Adam told you to attack a girl in a wheelchair?" Even Adam wouldn't stoop that low, would he?

"Adam told us to test you if we didn't believe him," Bull Guy said. "We did, and you failed."

"Why—"

Big Brody punched his ribs. Todd kneed him in the groin and sidled out of his grip, but Bull Guy grabbed his arm and shoved him into the wall, knocking the wind out of him. Before Todd caught his breath, his assailant punched his gut, right where Brody had hit him earlier.

Todd landed a blow to the guy's face, fist crunching through the cartilage in his nose, but by then Big Brody had recovered. He swung. Todd ducked, but the third guy lunged for him. He grabbed Todd by the hair and yanked. Todd kicked himself free, but Big Brody grabbed him from behind. He twisted Todd's arm behind his back and held him still.

Bull Guy lay on the ground, clutching what remained of his nose after Todd's punch pushed his piercing into it. Sweatshirt Guy smirked as he closed in. Todd was surprised not to see sharp teeth in that grin.

"Joey doesn't play nice with guys that don't follow orders."

"If Joey sends lackeys after girls, he doesn't deserve to give orders." Never mind that Minh had won that exchange; Todd disapproved on principle. Wasn't that what decent human beings did?

Sweatshirt Guy drew his arm back, but someone else's fist crashed into his face. Todd took advantage of the distraction and bucked, breaking free of Brody's grip. He whirled to find Maite had joined the fray. Shit. He couldn't defeat four of them.

It took him a moment to realize Maite was fighting on his side. Bull Guy figured it out faster and returned to the fight. Todd pushed him away from Maite, and soon he and Claire's friend were fighting back to back.

The guys may have bested them if Maite hadn't had self-defense training. She knew where to hit, and she directed her blows with the precision of a surgeon. The smaller guys ran off first. Big Brody glared at Todd before following.

Todd would have collapsed with relief, but he didn't want to appear weak in front of Maite. He still didn't know why she'd helped.

"Thanks," he said, hoping to draw out her motives.

Maite scrutinized her knuckles, perhaps trying to determine whether the blood was hers or Bull Guy's.

"I hate fighting people with nose rings."

"So why did you?" Todd said, too tired to be circumspect.

Maite pulled her water bottle from her backpack and rinsed her hand. "Betty's sister said you will need help."

"Betty's sister?" Beth. "Oh, you mean Minh?"

Maite nodded. "She said something about you taking off your flip-flops?" She looked at Todd's sneakers.

"I think she meant I'm one of the good guys now."

"Oh. English is weird."

"I guess so." Todd ran a hand through his hair, wincing as he passed over a newly formed lump. "Thanks." This was unfamiliar territory. He didn't know how to behave when Maite wasn't threatening him.

Maite dried her hand on her shirt, scowling as blood sprang from a scrape. She gave Todd a long look.

"Is true—is it true? What Minh said about your shoes?"

It took Todd a moment to realize she was referring to his flip-flopping. He considered his answer, knowing she'd search it for falsehood.

"I'm trying."

Maite scrutinized him even more thoroughly than she had her hand. Todd didn't know whether to revise his answer or run, but Maite spoke before he decided.

"Abuela has pre-made bouquets for procrastinators." She struggled to pronounce the last word.

"Huh?"

"Clara likes flowers." She strode away, as if that answered his question. Belatedly, Todd realized it did. Maite had just given him the way back into Claire's good graces.

CHAPTER 21

Todd held the bouquet close as he hopped off the bus. He'd waited all night to confront his brother about yesterday's "test," but Adam hadn't returned home. Todd decided to sacrifice his art class study session in favor of catching a few hours of sleep, but his thoughts spiraled out of control. Unable to rest, he'd made an early trek to Flores de Fernanda instead.

He stifled a yawn as he entered art class, only ten minutes late despite his detour. With his luck, he'd end up sleeping through economics. I'm sure Claire will appreciate that.

Cathryn grimaced as he took his seat. "If you're trying to impress Claire, you may want to cover that bruise."

Todd touched what had been a lump on his temple yesterday. Must be a bruise today.

Cathryn pulled her makeup from her purse and gestured for him to scoot closer, but Todd balked.

"Men don't wear makeup."

"They do if they don't want to frighten the womenfolk." Minh held out her hand. "Loan me a flower, will you? I'll make it into art."

Todd examined the mix of yellow roses, white lilies, and a red bloom whose name he couldn't pronounce. I suppose I can spare one. He handed a small rose to Minh.

"Aren't you going to ask about the flowers?"

Minh's expression said, "Duh." "I assume they're for Claire, unless my mad pepper spray skills earned me a not-so-secret admirer in the senior class."

134

"No, you're right." Todd allowed Cathryn to make over his bruise, figuring no one would notice makeup on his temple. He watched as Minh dusted the rose with gold and used it to dot patterns on her paper. "Thanks, by the way."

"For?" She snipped off a piece of the stem, rolled it in a blue powder, and rolled that over her paper.

"For sending Maite to help me yesterday. How did you know they'd come after me?"

"How didn't you?"

Todd blinked. She had a point. Wasn't he the "tough guy?" He'd participated in all of Adam's schemes. He should have expected trouble, but he hadn't predicted Adam's betrayal. Todd had always been a loyal sibling, trotting after Adam even when he walked straight into a fight. How could his brother have sent those guys after him?

Todd pushed aside his discomfort. He didn't mind engaging in legally questionable activities, but he wouldn't—couldn't—follow Adam if he attacked defenseless innocents. His cowardice in last year's incident with Saafi still haunted him, but he'd taken off his flip-flops, as Maite had put it. Adam must have an explanation. Otherwise...Todd would handle that later. For now, he'd focus on winning Claire back.

Todd spent the rest of art composing his apology to Claire. After Oliver dismissed the class, he shot out the door, forgetting to collect the loaned rose back from Minh.

The Gossip Girls, who were loitering outside the door to economics, chittered when they spotted him with the bouquet, but Todd marched straight to Claire's desk.

She sniffed the flowers, eyes full of suspicion. "A p-procrastination bouquet?"

"Actually, no. Maite's grandma said her pre-made ones weren't right for you, something about red roses being too strong and...there's a lot of symbolism to flowers."

Todd practically lived in the greenhouse, but floral art was a whole other world. Ms. Rojas had gushed about color balancing and complementary symbols. Todd hadn't understood a word, but the bouquet was beautiful. At least, it must be, because Claire hadn't tried to strangle him.

"Minh says you helped yesterday." Claire glanced at Beth, who nodded. Judging by Beth's expression, this wasn't the first time Claire had sought confirmation on the matter.

"Really? Because she told me I should have let her handle everything."

Beth chuckled. "Sounds like her." Her face sobered. "I can't believe I'm saying this, but thanks for looking out for her."

Todd couldn't remember the last time someone other than Noah thanked him. Part of him wanted to congratulate himself, but his rational side recognized the truth.

"It's like I said before. You don't have to worry about her. She can take care of herself."

Beth seemed about to respond to that, but Saafi cleared her throat. "Maybe we should work on our project and let Todd finish his apology."

"Right," Beth said. She scooted closer to Saafi, but neither pulled out their notebooks. They snuck glances at Claire and Todd.

"Subtle, guys," Claire said. She sniffed the bouquet. "About that apology?"

"Right. Uh, I'm sorry for what I said the other day. I was just trying to get Adam off my back."

"D-did it help?"

"It's a work in progress." Todd winced as his fidgeting twinged a bruise, suddenly grateful Cathryn had covered the one on his face. "Do you accept my apology?"

Claire stuck her face right against the flowers and inhaled. "It's a work in progress."

"Okay, then—"

The bell rang, and Todd's heart sank. He thought he'd have more time.

"Mr. Pohl's room," Claire said.

"Huh?"

"The guy who used to teach honors English? Mosaic is meeting in his room this week. Bring ssssomething cool."

Todd ought to feel thankful she didn't stuff the bouquet in the trash, but he couldn't help thinking girls were too much work. He brainstormed all afternoon, but what was he supposed to bring to represent his family culture? A box of condoms? His weed stash? *I'm sure Claire will love that.*

He was almost at his front door when his phone buzzed.

ADAM: Where are you?

Todd texted BUSY and bypassed his house in favor of the greenhouse. He wasn't sure he could confront his brother without punching him. Why would Adam have approved that attack?

Fifi greeted him, chewing on the new toy Todd had made. His bruises complained as he crouched, but Fifi's happy kisses made the effort worthwhile. At least someone was always happy to see him. Why can't people be more like dogs?

He stood, surprised to notice someone had rearranged the planters. Mrs. Thompson sat in a reclining chair in one corner, reading while Noah worked. She spotted Todd and grinned.

"I decided if I must spend so many hours sitting, I may as well rest among the plants I love."

Todd grinned. He understood completely.

She pointed to a nearby folding chair. "Come chat with me before my son puts you to work."

Todd gingerly lowered himself onto the chair, earning a quizzical look from Mrs. Thompson.

"You okay?"

Todd grimaced. "School is complicated."

"Anything I can do to help?"

Todd thought of his brother, Joey and his minions, Claire and her friends...What should he bring to Mosaic?

"Could you help me invent a new family history? I have to bring something that represents my culture."

Mrs. Thompson wrinkled her nose. Todd and Adam had never explicitly discussed their family life, but she'd had enough interactions with their mother to get the gist.

She pulled her walker in front of her chair. "Follow me."

She wobbled as she walked. Todd followed, arms outstretched to catch her if she fell. She navigated into the house with painful slowness, which may have been safer, but it only made Todd more nervous. He wanted her safely seated, now.

Transitioning from the kitchen tile to the living room carpet proved treacherous. Her walker hitched on the threshold, but she made it through. Todd breathed a sigh of relief as she settled into the soft chair.

She held out a pretty pot to him. "Take this."

Todd examined the small plant. It must be a perennial overwintering in the rosette stage of growth—small stem, six to eight leaves. Todd didn't recognize it from the greenhouse inventory.

"What is it?"

"A thistle."

Todd snorted, but Mrs. Thompson's gaze was serious.

"The thistle has served as an important symbol in Scottish heraldry for over five hundred years."

"You're Scottish?" She didn't speak with an accent.

Mrs. Thompson nodded. "My parents came to this country before I was born, but I've always liked thistles. They're tough."

Todd regarded the plant. It survived in harsh climates by defending itself with prickly spines, but it still attained some nobility, at least among the Scots. He felt a strange sense of kinship with the plant.

"You're sure I can take this?"

Mrs. Thompson nodded. "Keep it. I have another in my bedroom."

"Thanks." With a meaningful item to share, Todd could look forward to Mosaic. His phone buzzed.

ADAM: We need to talk.

Todd stared at the text, the implied threat hitting him like a knife in the back.

"Everything all right, Todd?"

"Can I sleep here tonight?"

Mrs. Thompson grinned. "Take the couch this time."

CHAPTER 22

Todd's plan to avoid his brother was simple: don't smoke. Adam would never search for him in class where he was supposed to be, so if Todd avoided his locker and his usual smoking spots, he'd be fine.

Minh raised an eyebrow as he set the potted plant on the art table. "Claire must have lowered her standards."

"The thistle is for Mosaic, which I noticed you don't attend."

"I hang out with my sister enough at home." Minh dabbed her brush into a blob of blue acrylic paints.

"And I work at the library after school," Cathryn said quietly. "Besides, I have to be home by dinner." Her next words came in a hurried rush, as if she were eager to change the subject. "Thistles are an important symbol in Scotland. Legend has it they even saved the Scots from a Viking invasion."

"Really?" Todd had been hoping to review for his next civics test, but a Viking invasion story would be perfect for Mosaic.

Cathryn nodded. "The stories say the Vikings tried a stealth attack that involved walking barefoot, but they trod on the thistles and cried out, alerting the townsfolk to their presence."

"Huh. Cool." Todd's affection for the plant grew. If a weed saved lives, couldn't he become a "decent human being?"

"Cat, we need to find you a boyfriend." Minh added thistle-like spines to the monster she was painting. Todd hadn't heard the day's prompt, but it never seemed to matter. Oliver liked everything Minh did, and as long as Todd and Cathryn spouted a moderately coherent explanation of how they'd contributed, they inherited her good grades.

139

As predicted, Cathryn was ahead on his civics studies, and she reviewed the test information with him for the rest of class. Todd absorbed the information easily, as if his brain were a muscle he'd been building, and now it could lift more weight than before. He even took notes in economics, much to Mr. Patel's surprise. He stopped the lecture once, thinking Todd was passing notes. When Todd showed him the notebook, his expression was priceless, and Claire shot him an approving smile.

"What's that?" she asked after Mr. Patel dismissed them to project work.

"You told me to bring something for Mosaic. The thistle is an important symbol of Scottish heraldry. It even saved the people from a Viking invasion." Claire rewarded him by leaning closer.

"I didn't know you were Scottish."

Todd shrugged. "I don't know if I am. Mrs. Thompson gave it to me."

"Who?"

Todd didn't want to delve into the gritty details of his childhood, but he didn't want to lose Claire's interest either. He settled on the Cliffs Notes version.

"My mom and I don't get along. Mrs. Thompson helped raise me."

"And your dad?"

Todd's saliva thickened, and he muttered his next words. "He's not a part of my life."

Claire rested her hand on his stubby fingers, and the touch drew Todd's eyes to hers.

"You never told me that."

I didn't want you to know. "You didn't tell me your mom had died until this year."

Claire withdrew her hand. "I g-g-guess we don't know each other as well as we thought."

"I'd like to change that." Todd put his hand, the injured one, on her arm. He waited for her to brush it aside, but she met his gaze instead.

"Okay."

They chatted for the rest of economics. Claire told him about helping the vet deliver a baby cow, and he described coaxing Fifi out of a customer's trunk. The more they talked, the more common interests they discovered. They both enjoyed quirky animals, long summers, hard workouts, and good food. Neither appreciated being the center of attention, especially not the drama that enthralled the Gossip Girls. Todd sensed Claire would prefer to live in peace, but she had enough backbone to fight if provoked. He'd always found her spunk attractive, but learning how she battled feeling insecure about stuttering heightened his respect for her perseverance.

They made zero progress on their project, but Todd had never felt closer to asking her out. He earned strange looks carrying a thistle around all day, but Todd trusted Adam wouldn't stoop to asking the Gossip Girls for help locating him. Lunch would have proven tricky if Mrs. Thompson hadn't sent him with leftovers. He snuck into the library to eat them, knowing Adam would never look for him there.

At last, the final bell rang. Todd hurried to the meeting room and boldly sat next to Claire. He explained the thistle's meaning for the third time that day, and his classmates shifted from outright hostility to cautious curiosity. All but Jeff Chen.

"You're Scottish?" Jeff said, skepticism evident in his tone.

"Well, I don't know, but—"

"Wait," the girl next to Jeff said. "You brought an important symbol from Scottish culture when you're not even Scottish?"

Saafi held up a placating hand. "I'm sure—"

"This group is for sharing cultures, not appropriating them," another girl said.

"Yeah, he can't do that," a guy said.

Not even Saafi's peacekeeping skills staved off the ensuing argument. Todd's classmates had been hunting for an excuse to reject him, and they pounced at this proof of their preconceptions.

"Okay." Todd stood, and the group fell silent. "You win. I'm leaving." He grabbed his thistle, tempted to trash it, but the plant didn't deserve his scorn. He tucked it under his arm and slammed the door behind him.

What was I thinking? No matter how many interests he and Claire shared, they couldn't bridge their differences. Claire was a heroine. He was a villain. Claire's family had always loved her. His parents had never wanted him. Gift baskets and flowers couldn't expunge his taint. Claire and her friends would never accept him. No one would.

"Todd, wait." Claire trotted after him, but Todd whirled.

"Forget it, Claire. You can open your restaurant with whatever perfect boyfriend you find in there." He gestured to the classroom. "I'm done."

She grabbed his arm, but he pushed her away so hard she fell. He didn't offer to help her up.

Though the air only hinted at spring, Todd's anger blazed with the heat of a desert summer. He barely remembered the trek home.

Adam met him in the kitchen, his own face filled with fury. "How—"

Todd shoved him into the counter. "Why did you send those goons after me?"

Adam's face registered shock and something else. Fear? They'd wrestled before, but now Todd had a pronounced physical advantage.

If Adam was afraid, the feeling didn't last long. His face hardened. "Those goons told me you're on their side, that you fought with Maite for fuck's sake."

"Not anymore," Todd growled as he trudged upstairs to their room. Adam followed, but his voice softened.

"What happened?"

Todd set the thistle next to the dead marigold. "You were right. I'm through with Claire."

"I tried to tell you." Adam's bed creaked as he dropped into it. "It's just us against the world."

"Yeah. You're right." Claire rejected him after every mistake, but Adam would always fight beside him.

Todd considered his two plants. Despite his tender care, the beautiful marigold had withered and died, but the spiny thistle survived in the harshest environments.

If Todd wanted to survive in this world, he'd have to grow thorns.

CHAPTER 23

Todd lay in bed trying to scrape the useless civics vocabulary out of his brain, but Cathryn had taught him too well. Definitions sprang into his mind, as if his brain knew he should be taking a test today.

Only a couple of days had passed, but Todd was already restless. He hadn't realized how thoroughly he'd altered his habits to pursue the impossible. He woke in time for art class, and even when he worked in the greenhouse, the urge to study whined in his mind like a caffeine craving. Though he hated to admit it, he missed the structured school day. He missed seeing what new idea Claire had concocted for their restaurant project.

Todd shoved his blankets—and his thoughts—aside as angry shouts reached him from downstairs. The door muffled the words, but he recognized the voices.

He threw a pillow at his brother's sleeping form. "Adam."

Adam groaned and rolled over.

Todd chucked a shoe at him. "Adam."

"Huh?" Adam batted away Todd's prodding.

"Dad is here."

"What?" Adam said, bleary eyes clearing. "What is he doing here?"

"Let's find out." Todd crept down the stairs. Adam must get his pacing habit from their mother, because her heels clicked as she traveled between the kitchen and the entryway. Their father stood inside the door, arms crossed over his chest.

"I have a right to them."

"You gave up that right when you paid me off."

"There is more to fatherhood than money."

"Oh, now you want to be a father." Their mother approached him, wielding her long fingernails like knives. "You think you can neglect them for eighteen years, then swoop in and steal them from me?"

Todd exchanged a glance with Adam. Their mother expressed less affection for them than the wicked witch had for Dorothy, but however paltry her parenting, she'd taken more ownership over their wellbeing than their father had.

"Spending time with them isn't stealing. I still have visitation rights."

"What do you mean?" Adam pushed past Todd and joined their mother. Todd groaned before following. Way to blow our cover.

Their father furrowed his brow, looking remarkably similar to the confused half of Minh's portrait of Todd.

"Shouldn't you two be in school?"

"Since when have you cared?" Adam shot back.

Their father puffed out his chest. "Since now. I've been talking with Shanice, my wife, your stepmom, and...I want to be more involved in your lives."

"Too little, too late," Todd said.

"Told you." Their mother hooked her arm through Adam's, but he shook her off.

"We don't want anything from you—either of you. We can take care of ourselves."

"If you're skipping school anyway, why not come over for lunch?" their father said. "You can meet Shanice."

"Why?" The word emerged with vitriol, but part of Todd genuinely wanted the answer.

His father blinked. "Because we're a family, and it's time we acted like one." He averted his gaze. "I wasn't ready for fatherhood when you were born, but watching Shantelle and Jayden grow up has made me realize how much I missed in your lives." He stepped toward them. "I know I hurt you, but please, give me a second chance."

Todd stiffened. "No one gave us a second chance." And he'd tried a lot harder than his father.

Ryan Easdon drew back. Adam strode to him with a cocky tilt to his chin, scanning him as though evaluating his fitness to parent. The man shifted his weight beneath the scrutiny. Regretting his invitation?

Adam shrugged. "It'd be a free lunch."

"You'll come?" Ryan directed the question to Todd rather than Adam.

Todd glanced at his mother, whose makeup ought to melt off her face given the steam exploding out of her ears. He echoed Adam's shrug.

"Hope your new wife is a good cook."

"Actually, I handle the cooking." He grinned goofily, but the boys' expressions must have told him how uncool it looked, because he cleared his throat. "Here's my address. Meet me at noon."

As soon as the door shut behind him, their mother shrieked. Her pacing increased in vigor, but she halted when her phone chirped.

"Peter, hi." She smiled sweetly, as if she hadn't just lost a battle with her ex. "No, I'm not busy. In fact, I was just thinking how nice it would be to meet you for lunch. What do you say? Perfect." She hung up and shot Todd and Adam a glare. "You're on your own."

"What else is new?" Adam said dryly.

Their mother didn't respond as she mounted the stairs, no doubt heading to change into a skimpier dress and add another layer of makeup. Adam followed her, but Todd paused. Should he feel guilty for hurting his mother's feelings? Whatever misgivings he had about her parenting, she at least tried. Should he have allowed his father to swoop in like that?

Todd shook his head. Adam was right. It was just a free lunch. Even if it turned into more—he couldn't keep his hope parasite from squirming at the thought—his mother had made her priorities clear, and they didn't include her children. Todd and Adam had a right to pursue a relationship with both parents, didn't they?

He returned to his room, where Adam added another pin to the family photo and tumbled back to sleep. Todd pulled out his laptop. Last year, his eavesdropping revealed his father's plans to buy them new computers, but his mother funneled the money to her personal trainer instead. She'd dated him until deciding relationships worked better when the man paid her.

Todd's nerves prickled as he pulled up his father's family photo—one free of Adam's tampering. He stared at the cheerful faces. Would his siblings look up to him, or would they consider him an invader into their perfect lives? There was a large age gap. Would they think of him as an uncle rather than a brother?

He couldn't expect their mother—his stepmother, he reminded himself—to welcome them. Then again, his father hadn't expressed more than a passing interest in them until he'd confessed to her. Was she directing this little reunion?

Was she the type who read her kids bedtime stories, kissed their scraped knees, and packed their lunches? Or was she more of a drill sergeant mom, demanding they finish their homework and chores before they had any fun? Todd couldn't tell based on the picture, but judging by her professional attire, she'd already started college funds for her kids.

His gaze shifted toward his father, whose smile looked more genuine than the ones he'd given Todd over the years. Ryan had shown his face at sporting events, and he dropped by the house to fight with Todd's mom, but they'd never spent quality time together. Did he snort when he laughed like Todd, or fidget when he was thinking like Adam? Did he know about his family history? What if Todd was Scottish?

Todd snorted. As if that would change anything. This meeting was doomed to failure. His father would measure him and, just like Claire and her friends, decide he wasn't enough.

Todd lay back to nap, but his hope parasite wiggled stubbornly inside him, keeping him awake. It reminded him of Fifi, who cheerfully greeted any new human who entered the greenhouse. A dog with her history should know better than to trust so easily, but her unconditional love for Todd spoke to her addled brain.

Todd's alarm sounded. Adam pretended to complain, but he hadn't been snoring. If he was nervous, however, he didn't show it on the drive over. They passed out of the city and through a first-ring suburb packed with small, cookie-cutter houses. They continued beyond that to a second-ring suburb with larger, more modern houses. Adam turned past an ornate brick sign that read BRIARWOOD.

Seeing the houses in his father's neighborhood, Todd was surprised there wasn't a gate blocking people like him and Adam from entering.

Each house portrayed a distinct style, but they all exuded the same presidential attitude, as if they were competing to become the next mayor's home. The neatly trimmed lawns weren't much bigger than the lots in town, but the houses swallowed the yards. Even the mailboxes had well-constructed brick housings.

"Guess we know how Mom funds her beauty treatments," Adam said. "They must charge Dad a fortune in child support."

They pulled into a driveway that was spotless despite the early spring slush that covered every roadway. Beyond the fence, an in-ground pool waited to be filled. A half-melted snowman stood in the yard, surrounded by toy shovels and soggy mittens. Todd smiled. Something about that hint of chaos in this hoity-toity neighborhood pleased him. His stepfamily seemed more human because of it.

They rang the doorbell, and Shanice opened the door. Wearing an expensive blue blouse and silver jewelry that highlighted her warm brown skin, she looked just as beautiful and put together as the photo portrayed her.

"You must be Ryan's boys," she said as she gestured for them to enter. "I'm Shanice."

Her tone was too formal to judge her feelings, but she gritted her teeth as Adam tracked dirty slush through her living room carpet. Todd stopped in the foyer to remove his shoes.

"I'm Todd." He held out his hand. Shanice shook his right hand, but her eyes drifted to the short fingers on his left. Had his father told her how he lost them? Did he even know?

They followed Adam's tracks to the kitchen, where Todd's father stood over a grill pan.

"Shame it's still too cold to grill," he said. "I'm a wizard with barbecue."

"Why don't I show you boys to the dining room while your father finishes lunch?" Shanice maintained her formal tone. Todd hoped she didn't always talk like that. At least his own mother was upfront with her emotions.

Only a ritzy neighborhood sported houses so large you needed a guide to reach the dining room. China cabinets lined the walls; their shelves filled with crystal, silver, and fancy plates he doubted they used more than twice a year. Four place settings graced the large mahogany table, with silverware laid out on neatly folded napkins.

"Where are the kids?" Todd asked as he and his brother took their seats.

"At school. It's best to keep this between us four for now." For the first time, her tone revealed her attitude. She clearly wanted to omit those last two words.

They sat in an awkward silence until Ryan appeared with an enormous platter in his hands and an even bigger grin on his face.

"Raspberry balsamic glazed grilled chicken breast with spicy roasted bell peppers, a tossed salad, and dinner rolls from that French bakery downtown."

"Spicy, sweet, and savory with a variety of nutrient groups." Todd didn't realize he'd said the words out loud until his father's goofy grin spread to clown-like proportions.

"You must have inherited my love of cooking."

"Uh, no. My...I had a friend once who liked cooking." Todd couldn't help wishing he were back in Claire's kitchen, chopping vegetables with her instead of fidgeting with his napkin ring.

"Oh." His father's face fell as he distributed the food. Conversation took a blissful break as they consumed their first bites. The food was good, but the awkwardness tainted Todd's tastebuds.

"So, what are you boys into?" Ryan asked.

"The usual," Adam said. "Drugs, sex, rock 'n roll."

Shanice dropped her fork. Her hand shook, though from fear or rage, Todd couldn't tell.

"I work at a greenhouse," Todd said. Adam nudged him under the table, as if they were only supposed to share their less wholesome hobbies. Todd mentally kicked himself. He'd spent all year trying to prove he could be a decent human being, and he'd received nothing but rejection. Now here he was, trying to earn his father's approval. So much for growing thorns.

"Really?" his father said around a mouthful of chicken. "Shanice is the director of marketing at a national horticulture company."

Shanice communicated much more with her eyes than she did with her tone. The glare she shot Todd's father said she didn't approve of the comparison. She wanted no common ground with Todd.

"Todd has two green thumbs," Adam said. "You should see him tend a marijuana plant."

The two adults ate their food with stiff movements.

Ryan cleared his throat. "How is wrestling?"

"We're not in sports anymore," Todd said.

"What? I gave your mother—"

"We used the money to get tattoos," Adam said. "I have a half-naked lady on my ass. Todd has a skull."

Shanice launched herself out of her chair and fled the room. Todd's father held up a finger and followed her.

Adam cackled like a crazed hyena. He pounded the table, making the silverware jump. Todd shook his head. He didn't have a tattoo, but if he got one, it wouldn't be a skull or a half-naked lady. He tiptoed after his father.

"Where are you going?" Adam said when he recovered his breath.

"Don't you want to know what they're saying?"

"Oh, I can guess," Adam said, but he crept after Todd, hiding behind him as Todd planted himself around the corner from the kitchen.

"...they're teenagers. They're going to be a little lippy."

"I don't want them near my kids," Shanice said. This time, her voice shook with emotion. Todd had expected rage, but desperation transfused her words. She must be a bedtime-story-reading mom, terrified for her kids' safety.

"Shanice—"

"Don't." She held up a hand, and her lower lip trembled. "I tried. You asked me to try, and I tried. Now please, think about our children."

Ryan's face melted. "Todd and Adam are my children, too. I'll visit them at their house, or bring them lunch every week. The kids will never meet them."

"Todd and Adam are almost eighteen, Ryan. You think they'll listen to you?"

"Don't you remember being eighteen?" He shook his head. "God, I was so lost, and I had a relationship with my father."

Shanice circled the small space between the stove and the island. "You couldn't have taken care of this, you know, when she was pregnant?"

"I offered to pay for it. I even offered to drive her to the nearest clinic." He shrugged. "She said it was her choice, but sometimes I think she had them just to keep a hold on me."

Todd cringed. He'd always felt his vocal support of a woman's right to choose made girls more willing to sleep with him. Hearing his own father discuss it so casually, however, made his lunch—the lunch his father cooked him—sour in his stomach. What kind of parents did he have? His mother brought him into this world to keep hooks in her ex, and his dad served him grilled chicken while wishing he'd killed him in utero. Todd looked over his shoulder to catch Adam's reaction, but he'd disappeared.

"Exactly," Shanice said, drawing Todd's attention back to the kitchen. "It was her choice. They're her problem. You don't owe them anything."

Ryan leaned against the counter, taking in his wife's pleading expression. "You're right. It's too late for this."

Todd's hope parasite shriveled and died. Now he knew which parent had given him the cowardice gene. His father had caved to his wife's pleas with little resistance. Not that Todd blamed Shanice. He'd wanted to become worthy of dating Claire, but somehow, he'd become a guy mothers feared influencing their children. He was nothing more than a problem, someone else's problem.

Adam tugged his shirt and jerked his head toward the front door. He led Todd through a second living room, grinding the dirt from his shoes into the carpet as he went. Todd didn't bother tying the laces on his shoes. He wanted out of this house as fast as possible.

Adam maintained a white-knuckled grip on the steering wheel as he drove them home. His earlier amusement vanished.

"He leaves us with Mom for seventeen years, and then he's mad we turn out rotten?" Adam shook his head. "We can show him rotten." He glanced at Todd. "You in?"

The last time Todd accompanied his brother on a revenge mission, they'd misfired, but this was different. They had seventeen years of neglect to rectify, and Todd was tired of chasing decency. Everyone he tried to please rejected him. Everyone except Adam.

Todd rubbed his thumb along the tips of his shortened fingers, memories flaring to life at the touch. He'd woken up in the middle of the hallway after sleepwalking. His mother's boyfriend had left his wallet and keys on the side table. Todd had never seen the man. He knew only that the guy was loaded, and his mother was happy.

At ten, he'd still been naïve enough to believe one of his mother's boyfriends would become his father. He knew better than to peer into the bedroom, but peeking at the guy's driver's license photo seemed a safe way to satisfy his curiosity.

Nothing but the man's cocky smile alluded to his wealth. Otherwise, he appeared normal—buzz cut black hair, brown skin, and eyes that had the same gleam Adam's got before winning a video game.

"What are you doing?"

Todd jumped as the man appeared at his side, narrow-set eyes targeting him. The photo hadn't depicted the man's height—or strength. He grabbed Todd's wrist and squeezed until Todd dropped the wallet.

"Little thief!" He pressed Todd's fingers to the doorframe. Before Todd could stammer his defense, the man slammed the door so hard he broke the hinges. The old wood splintered on contact, and pain lanced through Todd's hand.

"Hey!" Adam, awakened by the noise, grabbed a wooden shard and jabbed it into the man's arm. He growled.

"What's going on?" Todd's mother appeared in the doorway, half-dressed.

"You tell your little minions to steal from me?" The man didn't bother removing the shard before he shoved Adam into their room. He grabbed his things from the table and strode to the stairs, blood dripping onto the carpet. "We're over."

"Damien, wait." Todd's mother yanked her shirt over her head and rushed after him, but she stumbled over Todd. "Look what you've done," she said as she righted herself and followed her now ex-boyfriend down the stairs.

Todd liked to believe she hadn't known he was injured, that she hadn't heard him crying or seen him bleeding in the dark, but he was deluding himself.

After his mother left, Adam tended his wound. He plucked out the splinters with tweezers and wrapped Todd's fingers as best he could, but the bones were sticking out at odd angles. Their mother returned early in the morning, drunk, and stumbled to her bed. By then, Todd had a fever. Adam waited for their mother to wake, but she never left her room.

Todd didn't remember the rest, but he'd heard the story secondhand. When Todd was so delirious he couldn't see straight, Adam dragged him to the neighbors' place, and Mrs. Thompson brought them to the hospital. She signed the forms, claiming to be their grandmother. By the time their mother showed up, feigning sorrow and saying she would "fire that babysitter," the doctors told her they had to amputate Todd's fingertips.

She'd complained for weeks about how expensive that surgery was, and she'd blamed Todd for her boyfriend's refusal to take her back. When she found a new boyfriend, she mostly forgot the incident, but Todd never trusted her again.

Adam, he trusted. Adam had saved his life, and even when Todd had tried to break away from him, Adam welcomed him back without question. All these people who claimed to be "decent human beings" did nothing but reject Todd, while Adam, a "bad influence," stuck by him. Maybe Adam wasn't the bad guy after all.

"Todd, you in?" Adam repeated as they pulled up to their house.

Todd met his eye. "Ready when you are."

Chapter 24

This time, Todd added black gloves to his dark attire, hoping his father's security cameras wouldn't capture enough detail for anyone to notice the floppy tips on his left hand. Feeling self-conscious, he slipped into the passenger seat.

"Did you see his security system?"

"Don't worry," Adam said. "I disabled the alarm and stole a garage door opener while you were eavesdropping."

Todd's chest tightened, but he pushed the discomfort aside. It made little sense to feel guilty about stealing a garage door opener when you were about to vandalize the property.

Adam dumped a packet of white powder into his hand and snorted it through a straw before Todd could react.

"What are you doing?"

Adam grinned. "Just a little warm-up. You want some?"

"No." One of them should stay clearheaded. Todd's insides twisted as his brother sniffed again before driving away from the curb. Adam claimed he wanted to be a dealer, but his provider was turning him into a customer.

A light turned red. The car slipped as Adam braked, but he turned into the skid and righted it before they reached the intersection. Spring warmth melted the snow during the daytime, but night still clung to winter's chill. The highway was an ice rink.

Again, Todd wondered at the lack of a gate blocking his father's neighborhood. Maybe they'd build one after tonight.

"Shouldn't we park around the block?" Todd asked as Adam parked beside their dad's yard.

"Nah." Adam opened the garage door and hustled across the lawn.

Todd followed, but he tripped over something and fell into the refrozen slush. He cursed as pain and cold seeped into his knees. The clouds parted for a moment, and moonlight revealed what tripped him: the kids' snowman. His guilt returned. Destroying his dad's stuff was one thing, but the kids lived here too. This is a bad idea.

"Todd," Adam called from the garage.

Todd hoisted himself up and joined his brother, who stood between an SUV and a sedan that cost more than an entire row of cars in the school parking lot. Their glossy paint gleamed in the garage light. Adam grinned and handed him a golf club. As soon as Todd accepted it, Adam smashed the windshield of the bigger vehicle.

The garage light caught the creases in Adam's grin, giving him a maniacal look as he hit the SUV repeatedly. Todd stared at his own club, trying to summon his brother's courage. His father had chosen his new family over him. He'd believed a lunch date would absolve seventeen years of absentee parenting, and he'd dismissed his sons when even that required too much effort.

Todd tightened his grip on the handle and swung, smashing the sedan's windshield with a satisfying crash. Sweet, sweet revenge coiled around his spine and spread through his muscles. He swung again, taking out the side mirror. Again and again, he hit the car—once for every Father's Day, every birthday, and every Christmas his father had missed. He continued, rage expanding to include every time the principal called him "son," and every time his mom's boyfriend left a mess in the bathroom.

The car's front crumbled, but Todd wasn't finished yet. He hit the trunk too, once for every time he'd thought about holding Claire's hand, every time she'd given him that disappointed look. He didn't need her. He would never need anyone again.

By the time he destroyed the car's rear end, his muscles ached, but Adam was just beginning. His body vibrated with a crazed intensity, and he looked like a stranger. An angry stranger.

"Come on," Adam said, entering the house.

Thinking of those china cabinets, Todd followed, but his brother headed toward the stairs. Todd caught his arm.

"What are you doing?"

Adam's face shifted from manic to dark, as if someone had flipped a switch. "Shanice was so worried about her precious children..." He stepped toward the stairs, but Todd yanked him back.

"You're going after the kids? Are you insane?" Todd struggled to lower his voice to a harsh whisper.

"Those aren't just any kids, Todd. Can't you see? They're our replacements." He yanked his arm loose from Todd's grip, but Todd blocked his access to the stairwell.

"They're kids."

"Kids Dad chose over us."

"That's not their fault." Todd thought of the snowman outside. "Come on, let's smash the china and go home." Todd pushed him toward the dining room, but Adam stood his ground.

"When did you become such a pansy?"

When did you become a maniac? Todd shook his head. He didn't know who this insane person was, but it wasn't the brother who used to sneak him extra food.

"I am not hurting little kids, Adam."

Adam paused. Was he seriously considering it?

"Adam!" Todd tried to keep his voice down, but panic encroached on his self-control.

Adam shook himself, as if casting off dark thoughts. "We'll break their stuff."

Adam pivoted, bypassed the dining room, and entered a playroom. The cleanliness inside suggested Shanice applied the same rigor to her parenting that she did her career, unless Todd's father had dual personalities. Adam grabbed a giant teddy bear and ripped off the head.

Bile rose in the back of Todd's throat. "Adam..."

"Our whole lives, they've had everything we should've had." Adam swept his arm to include the entire room. "This is justice." He smashed a toy truck.

Todd scanned the room. Toys of all types—electronics, blocks, stuffed animals—rested neatly on shelves or in bins. As a kid, he'd longed for squirt guns and board games, but he and Adam had invented their own games with sticks and washed-out ice cream buckets. Adam was right. These kids had everything.

Todd lifted a box of train tracks, but his hands refused to destroy it. He loathed his father, but he'd rather help his half-siblings build a train track than make them cry by destroying it. Todd's childhood sucked, but he didn't wish it on them.

Todd returned the box to the shelf. "Adam, this is too far. Let's just break the china."

"No, Todd," Adam said darkly. "That's your problem. You don't fight for yourself. You never have." He handed Todd a video game console. "Break it."

Todd set it aside. "No."

Adam shoved the console back into his hands. "Stop letting him control you, Todd. He never wanted us, and he doesn't deserve us. It's us against them. Pick a side."

Pick a side. Like Big Brody's "test." A ball of heat flamed in Todd's chest. He set the console on the shelf.

"I'm not siding with someone who picks on little kids."

Todd should have read his twin's intent in the crazed gleam in his eye, but he didn't see the punch coming. He doubled over as Adam's fist connected with his gut. Adam elbowed his head, and Todd's ears rang.

Todd shook off his disorientation and shoved his brother into a cabinet. The shelves collapsed.

"No way they slept through that. Let's go." Todd left the playroom, but Adam leaped to his feet and rammed Todd into the living room wall. Todd kneed him, but he missed his brother's groin. He twisted Adam's arm to dislodge himself, but Adam punched his ribs. Todd grunted and kicked his brother to the floor, but Adam's flailing leg connected with Todd's newly bruised knees, and he fell.

The two boys wrestled, not stopping even after a siren blared. Todd pinned his brother, but Adam ripped off Todd's mask, scraping his face and eyes as he did. Todd cried out, and Adam wiggled out from under him.

"What's going on?" Their father stood at the top of the stairs, holding a hammer over his shoulder like a baseball bat. "Todd? Adam?" His shock tore something inside Todd, but he didn't have time to respond.

Adam howled and shoved Todd aside. He pounded toward the stairs, but Todd grabbed his ankle and yanked, bringing his brother to the floor again. Adam kicked his wrist, forcing his release. He lunged toward the stairs again.

"Police!" The front door burst open, and uniformed officers poured inside, guns drawn—and pointed at Todd.

Todd dropped to his knees and put his hands behind his head like he'd seen in movies. Adam fought, but two officers subdued him. Cold metal closed around Todd's wrists as an officer moved his hands behind his back. The officer was saying something, but a different sound caught Todd's attention.

"Daddy?" A little girl poked her head around his father's—her father's—legs. The boy next to her cried, but she stared at Todd in wide-eyed horror, as if he were a monster from one of her bedtime stories.

The officer pushed Todd outside. Patrol car headlamps illuminated the yard, highlighting the smashed snowman as Exhibit A.

His half-sister was right. He was a monster.

CHAPTER 25

Todd had never been arrested, but he hadn't imagined the process involved this much paperwork. The police shuffled him around, and everywhere he ended up, some tired officer asked him questions and filled out forms. No wonder TV shows focused on shootouts and high-speed chases. Who wanted to watch crime-fighting pencil pushers?

They separated him and Adam, or they tried to. Adam shot Todd looks he couldn't read as they were ushered into separate rooms. Todd sat in the plastic folding chair, thinking even the principal's office was more comfortable.

He recognized the two officers who joined him. The short Latina woman, Quintero, and her tall blond partner, Johansen, had questioned him at school after Adam's first foray into dealing.

"Shouldn't I have a lawyer?"

"Only if you're being charged with a crime," Johansen said.

"I'm not being charged?"

Quintero shrugged. "Lawsuits are hazy when minors commit crimes against someone who is technically still responsible for them. Your dad could file charges against your mom for failing to prevent you from committing the crime, but since he still has visitation rights..."

"We called your mother." Johansen's voice dripped sympathy. "She said she wouldn't pay bail, and jail would keep you out of her hair."

Todd's blood drained from his head, making him dizzy. I'm going to jail? "I-I thought I wasn't—"

"You're not," Quintero said. "And even if you were, we don't detain minors. We'll release you to your father's custody, unless your mother shows up to claim you."

"You're sending me home with the man whose house I just vandalized?"

Quintero leaned forward. "Kid, your file is awfully thick considering you've never formally been charged with a crime. I'd count my blessings if I were you."

She stood, gesturing for Todd to precede her out the door. He met Adam in the lobby, where their father waited. Ryan's face had acquired more lines in the past twenty-four hours. He jerked his head toward the door.

"Come on, you can work off the damage you've done."

Todd couldn't stand the thought of facing that little girl—his little sister—again, but to his shock, Adam slipped wordlessly into the waiting cab. He gave Todd the silent treatment the entire ride.

Their dad paid the cabby and gestured to the house. "You'll have to sleep on the living room floor tonight."

Adam stepped inches from his face. "Fuck you." He pushed his father away and stormed to their car, which was absurdly still parked beside the lawn.

"Come on, Todd. Let's go home."

Todd looked from his brother to his father. In one night, he'd betrayed them both. They were both offering him forgiveness, but Todd knew which one meant it.

He joined Adam in their car. On the way home, he watched the rearview mirror for flashing lights, but his father must not have called the cops again. His sons were lost causes.

"What happened to you?" Adam said.

Todd leaned his head against the cold window, exhausted from...everything. "I can't do it anymore, Adam. I'll grow weed, but you handle the dealing and vandalism, okay?"

Adam didn't answer. When they reached home, he dropped into bed and immediately started snoring. Tired as he was, Todd couldn't sleep. *What happened to me?* Striving for decency had shifted something in him. Now there were lines that he wouldn't cross, couldn't cross, but he still wouldn't fit in with Claire and her friends.

Was there room in this world for an imperfect person? One who couldn't be called decent, but wasn't a monster either?

Todd tossed and turned until sunlight slipped through the blinds. His restless legs drove him out of bed and over to the greenhouse. He considered napping in Mrs. Thompson's recliner, but he bedded down in his usual spot next to the heater. This time of year, they only needed it at night, but it was still running when his head hit the makeshift pillow made from canvas bags.

He'd barely closed his eyes when Fifi licked his face. He brushed her away, but Noah stood over him.

"Follow me." He passed into the house, Fifi at his heels. Todd dragged his tired body up the stairs. Noah led him to a small room and sat on a neatly made bed.

"This is for you." His gesture included the entire room.

Even sleep-deprived, Todd understood Noah's particular speech pattern, but he struggled with the man's meaning.

"What?"

Fifi jumped onto Noah's lap, and he patted the dog before answering. "Mom is sick. More sick. I need help. You can live here, rent-free, and work full-time." He held up a finger and placed heavy emphasis on his next words. "If you finish school and stay out of trouble."

Todd leaned against the wall, propping himself upright as his legs gave out. Noah's offer would allow him to escape his mother's house, extricate himself from his brother's schemes, and work a job even Claire would approve of, but that if...

Todd sank to the floor. "I can't—"

"Yes, you can," Noah said. "I believe in you."

Todd met Noah's gaze, but no hints of sarcasm appeared in the man's flat-featured face. "You wouldn't say that if you knew where I'd been all night."

"I don't need to know where you've been. I know who you are."

Todd snorted. "And who am I?"

"A good guy."

160

The words unlocked a dam in Todd, as if he'd waited his whole life to hear them. I'm a good guy. His eyes watered, and he couldn't keep the tears from flooding his cheeks. He didn't have to be a vandal who attacked his own family and sought revenge for every slight. He could garden to his heart's content, using his strength to serve people instead of hurt them.

Fifi leaped onto his lap and licked away his tears. Todd patted the dog. Noah had a way with strays. Fifi had turned out okay. Maybe there was hope for him.

"You want the room?" Noah asked when Todd looked up.

Todd hesitated, unwilling to betray Noah's trust the way he had everyone else's. He'd chosen the honors track to win Claire, but he'd quit school after realizing he'd never meet her standards. Now he had another reason to study. Principal Evans's words came back to him. "You may have joined for a girl, but you'll stay for yourself."

"Yeah." Todd almost laughed. "Yeah, I do."

Noah nodded, as if he'd expected that answer. "Get some sleep."

Todd collapsed onto the bed, not bothering to put himself under the covers. Even though daylight streamed through the curtains, it was the best night's sleep he'd ever had.

CHAPTER 26

Fifi's cold nose woke him. Todd groaned and rolled over, but the earth dropped out from under him. As his butt hit the hardwood, his foggy brain cleared, and he remembered he was in a bedroom instead of on the greenhouse floor. His bedroom.

Todd peered through the curtains at the light skimming the horizon—from the east. That can't be right. He'd gone to sleep at dawn. Had he slept for twenty-four hours?

An alarm clock blared, and Todd rushed to silence it. A muffin lay on a plate beside it, along with a note written in blocky uppercase letters. HAVE A GOOD DAY AT SCHOOL.

Todd smiled, unsure whether to be happy the sun hadn't started setting in the east or dismayed to have slept so long. At least he felt refreshed. Not ready to return to school, but he couldn't let the Gossip Girls' rumors, cranky teachers, and disdainful classmates keep him from pursuing the life he wanted. He'd wasted too much time already.

Todd crammed the muffin into his mouth as he straightened his rumpled clothing. He'd have to retrieve his things from home later, assuming this wasn't a practical joke. No. Noah didn't like practical jokes, a fact he and Adam had exploited in their younger days.

Adam. What would he tell Adam? Nothing he hadn't already said. He'd already restricted himself to growing the Ides of March. He could tend Caesar's plot and work full time at the greenhouse, but first he had to graduate, meaning he needed to get his butt to school.

Todd found the bathroom and splashed water on his face, wincing as the soap stung his cuts. He inspected the scabs in the mirror, but something green caught his attention. On the shelf behind him lay a T-shirt sporting the greenhouse logo. The note pinned to it read TODD in Noah's childlike handwriting.

At least I won't look like a bandit. He didn't know enough about fashion to determine whether a green shirt matched black pants, but he didn't care. After rinsing off last night's misadventure, he donned his new shirt and bounded down the stairs. He waved to Noah, who was already puttering about the house. Like many gardeners, Noah woke with the sun. Perhaps Todd would too someday.

More sunshine than usual lit his walk to school, a testament to the longer days and warmer weather to come. The air still held a chill, but it refreshed rather than bit. Todd wiggled through the familiar door. He'd only missed a few school days, but he felt as though he'd died of old age and been reincarnated as a teenager. He vowed to do better this time.

"Look who's back," Minh said as he joined her and Cathryn at the art table. "Cat and I took bets on whether we'd see you again."

Cathryn furrowed her brow. "I don't gamble."

"That's because you know I'm always right."

"You wagered I'd be back?" Todd said. "I would have thought you'd bet against me."

"You don't strike me as a delicate lily that wilts just because someone hurts your feelings," Minh said as she squirted a blob of green paint onto a newspaper. "You're more like a thistle—so hard to uproot that the gardener decides the flower is pretty and claims she planted it on purpose."

"Are you saying I'm pretty?"

"I can make art with anything." Minh grabbed his left hand, dunked his stubs into her paint blob, and used them to paint.

Todd laughed. He hadn't realized how much he'd missed art class silliness.

Cathryn cleared her throat. "You missed a civics test, and you're a full unit behind in math."

Todd raised his eyes to the ceiling. Couldn't she have waited five minutes before dropping that avalanche?

"Can you still tutor me?"

Cathryn smiled as if she'd been hoping he'd say that. "I had to stay home a few days this week, so I used the extra time to make study guides."

Minh's raised eyebrow suggested she thought Cathryn ought to get more fresh air, but in lieu of commenting, she plunged Todd's hand into a blob of blue paint. Todd allowed it, figuring he may as well participate in the art he was getting credit for. Cathryn outlined the content he'd missed, and though it overwhelmed him, he could finish it. He had to if he wanted to stay with Noah.

Todd didn't wait for Oliver to finish praising Minh's "embracing the human body for the tool it is" before hurrying to economics. Instead of scolding Todd from behind the lectern, Mr. Patel remained at his desk, his eyes slanted as if he resented the latecomer's distracting him from important business. He must have allocated the entire hour for project work.

Todd caught Claire's eye, but Beth greeted him first.

"How is Minh always right?"

"You bet I wouldn't come back?"

"After what Maite told us? I thought you'd gotten yourself killed."

Todd slowed, feet heavy as he reached his seat. "What did Maite tell you?"

Claire answered. "She said the p-p-p-Officer Johansen showed her your photo and asked whether you were the one who vandalized the shop."

"Oh. Right." So much for a fresh start.

"Todd, are you in trouble?" Claire gestured to the scratches Adam dug through his face.

Todd hesitated. "I was, but I'm done with that now. I even got a full-time job offer for after graduation." He pointed to his T-shirt.

"I never would have pegged you as a gardener," Saafi said. She and Beth were once again ignoring their project in favor of eavesdropping. Knowing those two, they were ahead anyway.

Beth gestured to Todd's hand. "Didn't know gardeners used that much paint."

Todd wiggled his stubs, showing off the lingering paint smudges. "Your sister welcomed me back by using me as a human paint brush."

Beth laughed. "I love that girl." The noise elicited a hiss from Mr. Patel, and she and Saafi refocused on their own project.

Claire cleared her throat. "I'm...I'm sorry about what happened in Mosaic."

Todd blinked, trying to remember the last time someone apologized to him. Claire had hurt him, and she knew it. Was this her asking for a second chance? How should he respond? A relationship with Claire was no longer his primary goal. He had his own life plans now, but could Claire take part in them? What if she rejected him again?

Todd had spent all year seeking absolution, but for the first time, he understood the burden of forgiving. He glanced at Saafi, overwhelmed by her courage.

"Todd?"

"Don't worry about it." Todd scooted closer to Claire, not knowing where this road would lead, but wanting to travel down it anyway. "Is it in a restauranteur's budget to install security cameras and shatter-resistant glass?"

"To sssssafeguard our vegetables?"

"I was thinking to protect your secret recipes, but..."

Claire chuckled. "I'm sure Maite would give us a c-consultation."

They decided a safe would prove more economical than shatter-proof glass, and they brainstormed additional security measures for the rest of class.

Todd spoke bluntly to his next teachers, acknowledging his late work but committing to finishing it. Remarkably, the majority agreed to give him extensions. Either they sensed his sincerity, or he was the only student on the honors track with late assignments, so his wouldn't create too much extra grading. A weird advantage, but Todd wouldn't complain. He'd never feared hard work, but now he committed to exercising his brain as well as his biceps. He wasn't sure whether the change in circumstances or the change in himself improved his attitude, but for the first time, he felt like he would survive high school. He had hope again, thanks to Noah.

Maybe all he'd needed was for someone to believe in him.

Todd strode through the cafeteria, disappointed that his usual table looked the same as always. With how different he felt, it should have been gold-plated. He dunked a dry chicken nugget in ketchup, wondering where Adam was. Had he officially dropped out? Most buyers of the Ides of March attended Brooks High. Why would Adam abandon his customer base? Todd hadn't schmoozed with the stoners lately, so Adam would have to handle the networking. Why wasn't he here? Was he still mad?

Before Todd finished his wild thoughts, Adam appeared, grinning as he plopped an extra chocolate milk next to Todd. They'd always eaten lunch together, but as with the unchanged table, the familiarity troubled more than it comforted, as if his brother brought a heavy shadow with him.

"I need you after school today," Adam said. "We are back in business."

"I'm not helping you deal anymore."

"What, because of last night?" Adam said around a mouthful of breaded chicken. "The cops caught us red-handed, and they still couldn't do anything. I figure we ought to take advantage of our lucky streak." He popped another chicken nugget into his mouth.

"I'm not worried about getting caught. I just don't want to deal." Todd pushed his lunch tray aside, no longer hungry.

Adam chewed slowly. "You're serious. What is with you? You never had a problem selling the Ides of March."

The Ides of March doesn't turn brothers into psychopaths. Did Adam even remember that night? Todd would never forget the crazed look in his twin's eye.

"We should stick to our strengths. I'll grow the weed. You handle the business. If you need someone to loom threateningly over your shoulder, ask Big Brody."

Adam's expression darkened more with every word that left Todd's mouth. "You—"

"And I need the car this weekend."

"What?" Adam's surprised gesture knocked over his milk. He didn't bother wiping up the spill.

"I need to haul some equipment to Caesar's."

Adam scanned him as if wondering whether Todd was an imposter. He wasn't used to taking orders from Todd, and judging by his expression, he didn't like it. Todd lifted his chin. Adam would have to accept his terms if he wanted Todd's help.

"Fine." Adam lurched to his feet, taking the extra chocolate milk with him.

Though the confrontation unsettled Todd, setting boundaries gave him the confidence to convince the rest of his teachers to accept his late work. He marched home, victory warming him enough that he wouldn't have needed his jacket even if he'd brought it. When he stepped through his back door, he was ready for his mother's ambush.

"Todd, I need you to—"

"No." He savored the word.

Her long, painted fingernails dug into her hip. "Excuse me? As long as you live under my roof—"

"Then I guess I'd better move out." Todd pushed past her, retrieved his things from his room, and left his childhood behind for good.

CHAPTER 27

Though his teenage body begged for more sleep, Todd hauled himself out of bed just after dawn. Noah passed him in the hallway, carrying a breakfast tray for Mrs. Thompson, who was still recovering from a cold that had hit her harder than the flu.

"There's extra in the kitchen, and I left you a list."

Todd grunted his good morning and found scrambled eggs and fruit for his own breakfast. He liked that the Thompsons always had real food, nothing from a box for them. The eggs tasted better than the toaster tarts he'd eaten at home. No, he reminded himself, this was home now.

He hadn't planned to read Noah's list, but he glanced at it as he munched. The usual tasks for transitioning seasons were scrawled in Noah's childlike handwriting, but the last item made Todd laugh. Noah had added HOMEWORK AND STUDYING to his chores.

His belly full, Todd launched into his work with gusto. The snow continued to melt, turning streets into streams and waking gardeners from hibernation. The greenhouse would be ready for them.

He zipped through his work faster than ever, as if his body were thanking him for sleeping better and smoking less. He grinned as his lungs filled with air scented with plant life. Maybe he'd give up smoking. If it kept his body in peak condition, it might be worth it.

He was hefting a pile of new planters up a ladder when a customer caught his eye. The woman appeared how Todd imagined Mrs. Thompson would if her disease hadn't aged her. She browsed the greenhouse casually, as if she had no intention of purchasing anything, but just wanted to enjoy her outing. Something near Todd must have caught her eye because she strode toward him, but she tripped before she reached him.

Todd leaped off the ladder and caught her before she hit the ground.

"Oh, dear, what a klutz," she said as she righted herself.

"Klutz? Here I thought you wanted to dance." Todd, who still held her hand, swayed side to side a couple of times. The woman laughed and twirled for show.

"Thanks, kid. You're sweet."

Todd smiled. "Let me know if you need help."

She waved away his offer and examined the seed catalogue. Todd returned to pulling planters up the ladder.

"I always admired that about you."

Todd jumped so high he knocked the ladder over, and plastic planters rained down on him. The customer glanced his way, but she must have concluded he already had help, because she returned her focus to the seed catalogue.

"Are you okay?" Claire picked her way through the fallen planters.

"What are you doing here?" Panic made his voice squeak. He felt more exposed than if a search light had caught him skinny-dipping. The greenhouse was his sanctuary, but Claire's presence whipped his emotions into chaos. Claire had rejected his attempts to redeem himself, and now she was evaluating the sapling of his new life. Would she give it water and sunlight or crush it beneath her boot?

"I thought maybe you'd lied about the job," Claire said. "Apparently not. Unless you're going to get fired for that." She pointed to a broken planter beneath Todd's thigh.

"I don't think so." Todd unburied himself and restacked the fallen planters, unable to meet her eye. "What did you mean when you said you admired me?"

"You find ways to save clumsy p-people from embarrassment. Don't you remember when we met?"

Of course. He'd helped her retrieve her fallen purse after she'd tripped up the stairs. "You still like strawberry-scented lip gloss?" He risked a glance. Mistake. Her smile made his head spin.

"Yeah." Her expression grew serious. "I was always so nnnnnnn-nervous about talking to you, but I d-didn't need to worry, did I?"

Todd shrugged. "I never cared if you stuttered. I was just glad you liked me." He shelved the last planters, hoping she didn't see the blush creeping into his cheeks.

A small yip sounded, and Fifi pitter-pattered to Todd.

"It's all right, girl." He picked her up and scratched behind her ear.

"Why am I not surprised you're a d-dog person?" Claire closed the gap between them to pet Fifi.

"I take it you're a cat person."

Claire grinned wryly. "I prefer cows."

She continued petting Fifi, shifting so close her shampoo's fruity scent wafted into his nose. He grinned. She really did like strawberries.

"Hey."

Todd and Claire jumped as Noah appeared beside them.

"No girlfriends at work."

"She's just a friend." Todd returned Fifi to the floor sheepishly. "She likes herbs."

"Then show her." Noah pointed to the table full of baby herb plants. Todd walked three steps toward it before he realized he'd taken Claire's hand. He dropped it, and Claire marched to an indoor planter, complete with a grow light for overwintering. She eyed the price tag, which declared the product on clearance.

With a thoughtful twist to her lips, she joined him at the herb table. She rubbed a leaf of basil between her fingers and sniffed her hand, closing her eyes. Her dreamy smile looked so peaceful Todd wanted to take a picture. Apparently, he wasn't the only one who took solace in plant life.

Claire opened her eyes and caught him staring, but instead of reprimanding him, she blushed.

"My mmmmom had an herb garden. We used to-to weed it whenever someone teased me for stuttering." Her eyes grew distant as she fingered a sprig of tarragon. "I know it's silly, but that always made me feel better."

"I don't think that's silly. Why do you think I come here?" Either the setting loosened his tongue, or Todd was losing his mind, because words he never thought he'd say tumbled out. "My dad never wanted us, and my mom burned through boyfriends like a chain smoker. Whenever things got bad at home, I knew Mrs. Thompson would feed me. Hell, I started sleeping here so often, Noah gave me my own room."

Claire studied him, and Todd ran a hand through his hair, wishing he could retract his words. This conversation was too intimate, his newfound confidence too fragile. Claire could destroy him with a glance.

"I don't know what to make of you, Todd." Claire spoke whisper soft. "One minute you're running from the police, the next you're gardening."

Todd forced himself to meet her eye. "Adam and I got into some messed up stuff, but I'm out." He gestured to the greenhouse. "This is the life I want. It's not cool or sexy or a big money maker, but I don't care. I just want to be happy."

There. He'd said it. He'd laid himself bare before her, but his nerves evaporated and his newly resurrected hope parasite took root. Let her reject him. Let her list all the reasons he'd never measure up and laugh at his feeblemindedness. He didn't need her approval to pursue his dreams.

"So Vandal Todd is gone, and Gardener Todd is sssssssticking around?"

Todd widened his stance. "Yes."

"Good. Because I like him better." Claire smiled coyly, and Todd struggled to breathe.

She peered over his shoulder. "Your b-boss is glaring at me."

Todd glanced at Noah, who was indeed squinting in their direction. "He's probably trying to figure out whether you're a bad influence."

"Oh?"

"Well, you do prefer cows to dogs."

Claire laughed. He'd forgotten how much he liked how her nose wiggled when she laughed.

"I'll have to prove myself, then." Claire glanced at the clearance display. "Do you think he'd give me a d-discount on that grow light if I help you finish your shift?"

"You want—"

"I grew up on a ffffarm, remember? I'm not afraid of a little dirt."

Todd grinned. "In that case, I'll see what I can do."

They laughed through the entire shift, but Noah accepted Claire as a good influence after they finished half the next day's to-do list. By the time Claire left, Todd thought he might float to the ceiling.

Adam's text brought him back to Earth.

ADAM: You finished with the car?

Todd stared at the message, feeling like a lasso was strangling his chest and pulling him toward his brother. He'd told Adam he'd set up Caesar's plot. They'd planned to start earlier this year to maximize Minnesota's short growing season, but Claire's arrival had pushed all thoughts of the Ides of March from his mind. Todd glanced outside. If he headed to Caesar's now, he wouldn't finish until well after dark, meaning he'd sleep through class tomorrow. If he stayed home, however, Adam would want to know why. He doubted Adam would approve of his spending the day with Claire.

ADAM: Everything set?

TODD: Noah had to order the row covers. I'll finish next week.

Adam would see through the lie eventually, but damage control could wait. Todd shoved his phone into his pocket and headed upstairs to finish Noah's last task: HOMEWORK AND STUDYING.

CHAPTER 28

T odd never thought he'd feel guilty for doing homework, but no amount of rehearsing his excuse for neglecting the Ides of March prepared him to face Adam. He wasn't avoiding his brother, but the more freedom he experienced in his new life, the less enthused he was about anything connecting him to the old one.

Todd sat in his usual seat at lunch, eating what might loosely be categorized as pizza. He expected Adam to materialize beside him, but his brother remained absent. Half of Todd was relieved, but the other half suffered a pang of guilt. He'd launched into a new life, but Adam was still his brother. He couldn't leave his twin behind.

"Todd." Claire held a large tray supporting a two-tiered cake. She jerked her head toward her friends' table. "Come join us."

She rejoined her friends, but Todd hesitated. Not even when they'd been flirting around last year had she invited him to sit with her. He approached the table cautiously, surprised the seat didn't electrocute him when he sat beside Claire.

"See, Maite. He's alive," Beth said.

Maite tilted her head. "Huh. Good."

"Good? I thought you hated me. What changed?"

Claire patted his shoulder. "Unlike Adam, you k-keep trying. We decided that's worth something." She lifted a dull knife. "Who wants cake?"

"What kind?" Saafi asked.

"Chocolate with d-dark chocolate ganache and white chocolate b-buttercream."

173

"What are we celebrating?" Todd asked. The white frosted cake didn't sport any writing.

Claire sliced a gigantic piece and heaved it onto Maite's tray. "Beth got into law sssschool; Saafi's going to med school; Maite got accepted into a c-criminal justice program, and it happens to be my b-birthday. I ffffigured since you got a job at the greenhouse, you deserved a slice too."

"It's your birthday?" Why didn't I know that? "Uh, happy birthday."

Saafi grinned. "Don't worry, Todd. Falis and I would be delighted to spend your money again. I'll get you her business card." She winked as Claire handed her a slice of cake.

If someone had told Todd that Saafi would offer to shop with him, he'd have told them to quit what they were smoking and buy the Ides of March. In the fall, she'd been kind but cautious. Now she was eating cake with him, but she wasn't the only one who'd revised her opinion of him.

Beth started the year warning him away from her sister, but after the pepper spray incident, she'd thanked him for looking out for Minh. Maite threatened to pummel him after seeing him at the greenhouse. Now she was glad the cops hadn't arrested him. Last year, Claire had given him a black eye and barred him from speaking to her, but now she'd invited him to sit with her at lunch.

He liked this strange upside-down world. Maybe it could become his new normal.

But it couldn't. High school would end soon.

"Claire, what will you do after graduation?" What if she attended college out of state? What if she met someone else? He'd finally earned her trust. Would he lose her so soon?

Assurance settled into Todd as his hope parasite rooted deeper within him. Even if she left, he'd still have Noah and the greenhouse. Claire was no longer a goal; she was a girl, one he enjoyed spending time with, but didn't need. Somehow that made him feel more worthy of holding her hand, as if he'd needed to be confident in his life before he could share it with her.

Claire dished him a piece of cake that rivaled Maite's. "I'm going to visit my grandparents for a few weeks, but my aunt says I can live with her while I'm in culinary school." She gestured to the cake. "Eat up. You wouldn't b-believe how hard I worked to C-onvince Mrs. Greiner to let me borrow the cafeteria fridge."

Todd took a bite, and a mixture of bitter dark chocolate and sweet white chocolate tantalized his tastebuds. The cake tasted like a new beginning.

His next classes passed smoothly. He'd thought his teachers had given up on him, but they accepted his first batch of late work with smiles and encouraging words. When the final bell rang, Todd decided to press his luck by asking to walk Claire to the bus. He strode to her locker, but just as he reached her, Adam stormed down the hall, his coat flapping behind him as if a blizzard were blowing it back.

"I should have known you'd be with her."

Claire set her feet. "Todd is old enough to choose his own friends."

Within moments, Beth, Saafi, and Maite flocked behind her, but Adam addressed Todd.

"Can't you see she's manipulating you?"

"By ssssaying it's wrong to break other p-people's property?" Claire said.

Todd stepped between them before Claire could antagonize his brother further. "I told you. I'm just tired of the drama."

"Do you even hear yourself? You're hanging out with those four, and you think I bring the drama?"

"Adam—"

"Open your eyes, Todd. She's a manipulative bitch like Mom, and you're falling for it like all Mom's doofus boyfriends." Adam leaned sideways to focus his glare at Claire. "Get your fangs out of my brother, or I'll yank them out."

"I'm nnnnot afraid of you." Claire's voice was low, almost a growl.

"'I'm C-c-claire, and I'm n-n-n-n-not sssscawed of you,'" Adam taunted.

Claire lunged, but Maite restrained her, tilting her head toward the crowd of witnesses.

"Go home, Adam," Todd said.

Adam grabbed his shirt. "If you don't meet me at the car in five minutes, you're no longer my brother." He shoved Todd aside and stalked away.

Todd threw Claire an apologetic look. "I'll see you tomorrow."

She lifted her chin. "Will you?"

Anger flamed in her eyes, but hurt lay beneath it. She was sick of wondering which half of Minh's Todd Portrait would show up. Todd wasn't either half anymore: neither the befuddled student nor the sinister monster.

He wasn't the insecure boy who trotted after his twin. He was master of his own garden now, and he'd uprooted the weeds and set the boundaries. Sharing his heart with Claire was a risk, but not the one Adam believed. Claire could hurt him, but she couldn't manipulate him. He wasn't a follower anymore. He was something else, something stronger, bolder.

Before his brain raised the logical objections to his next move, he stepped forward, took Claire's face in his hands, and kissed her. It wasn't the half-drunk, I-want-more kiss he'd given her in the past. It was a kiss that said, "I'll be here tomorrow, but I want you to know I love you today." To his relief, she returned it, taking a startled breath when they separated.

"You're supposed to ask me out before you do that," she whispered.

"Sorry, I'm still getting the hang of being a good guy." Todd smiled, and her freckled cheeks reddened. "I need to take care of Adam, but I'll see you tomorrow."

He left her to her friends' teasing giggles, feeling like he could march up a mountain if necessary, but he had only one hill to climb. He braced himself before joining his brother in the car.

"You need to dump that chick," Adam said.

"Actually, I'm going to ask her to prom."

The engine roared to life with extra sound as Adam revved it. "I'm not letting her tear us apart."

"Then I'm not growing weed for you."

Adam almost missed their turn as he stumbled through his reply. "You need it more than I do."

"Not anymore." Todd would build a life he didn't need to escape from. He didn't need Caesar, and he didn't need Adam's micromanagement. "Leave Claire alone."

Adam slammed the brakes. "Get out."

"Adam—"

"Get out!" His voice shook with rage and hurt.

"Adam..."

Adam fixed his gaze on the windshield. "She's scrambled your brains, Todd, but don't worry. I'll fix everything. Now scram. I have work to do."

"Adam, I don't—"

"If you won't help, leave."

Todd exited the vehicle, rubbing his short fingers as Adam drove away. For once, he didn't think of Adam in the remaining healthy stubs. He thought of the diseased tips he'd had to cut away to survive. Drugs, parties, smoking—Todd would quit it all, regardless of what Adam thought.

Adam planned to "fix everything," but it was his head that needed readjusting, not Todd's. When Adam inevitably caused more trouble than he could handle, Todd would pull him out of it. He may be ten minutes younger, but he was now the older brother. He'd give Adam some time to cool off, but he wouldn't let his twin settle for life as a criminal. No more avoiding confrontations. From now on, Todd would lead.

Todd strode back to the greenhouse, back home, knowing he'd never touch the Ides of March again.

Chapter 29

Todd checked his phone to confirm the text was real.

ADAM: We'll talk Friday.

After days of stonewalling, Adam finally agreed to meet. Why he wanted to meet tomorrow instead of today didn't matter. At least he'd agreed to talk. Todd had rehearsed his arguments all evening, but that wasn't the only pending conversation on his mind.

When he arrived in art, Minh already had her nose to the page, pens in hand. She didn't even greet him when he sat beside her. What he glimpsed through her hair involved an intricate linear pattern.

"Am I late?" Todd checked the clock.

"Cat spied on Oliver to get today's prompt ahead of time," Minh answered as she used a ruler to add a line.

"Reading the syllabus is not spying." Cathryn grimaced as she shifted her position.

"Are you okay?" Todd said.

Cathryn swallowed, and her cheeks reddened through her makeup. "I...may have tripped down the stairs."

Minh snorted. "Cat, I'm pretty sure I could take the stairs more gracefully than you."

"Thanks," Cathryn said flatly. She turned to Todd. "Do you want to cover civics or science first?"

"Actually, I was hoping for some...feminine advice from you two today."

Minh looked up from her drawing. "Oh?"

"I want to ask Claire to prom, and since I want her to say yes, I figured I'd better ask the experts." Three months ago, he hadn't cared a beetle's dung ball about prom, but now he couldn't stop wondering how Claire would look in one of those fancy dresses. He'd drunk his way through many parties, but he'd never just danced with a girl. I bet Claire is a terrible dancer. The thought made him smile.

"Try quoting Shakespeare," Cathryn said.

Minh slapped the table. "For the last time, Cat, not everyone loves Shakespeare."

Cathryn spread her hands. "Romeo & Juliet is the closest thing I've read to a romance novel."

"Don't they both die in the end?" Todd said.

"Well, yeah, but—"

"I rest my case," Minh said. She sketched something on a piece of scratch paper. "It's like that gift basket, but turn it into a question rather than an apology. Use some twist-ties to fasten a bunch of flowers and chocolate bars to a poster board in the shape of the word PROM."

She ripped off the sketch and handed it to Todd. Her thirty seconds of work created a professional looking card he could hand Claire that minute. How does she do that?

"You could include little scrolls with poems inside," Cathryn said. "I'll give you a list of poets."

Minh's hand hovered over her pens. "You read romantic poetry, but not romance novels?"

Cathryn shrugged. "Only poems written in the iambic rhythm. I like the way it highlights English syllable structure."

"Thanks," Todd said as Minh shot Cathryn another look demanding the bookworm leave the library more often. "These are great ideas."

"We accept compensation in chocolate form, so buy extra," Minh said.

"Will do." Todd owed these two more than chocolate for all their help. His mother hadn't raised him to write thank-you cards and other social niceties, but he would figure it out. He made a mental note to remind Saafi to give him Falis's business card. He had a lot of shopping on the horizon.

Todd made it to economics early and used the extra time to type Cathryn's list of poets into his phone. Just as he finished, Beth and Saafi entered the room. Their phones buzzed, and their faces grew serious as they read the text. As soon as they sat down, they started whispering.

Mr. Patel began lecturing before Todd could ask where Claire was. Saafi's and Beth's phones buzzed again. They read the texts, glanced at Todd, and typed their responses. What's going on?

"Ladies, if you won't pay attention, I'll confiscate your phones," Mr. Patel said.

"Sorry," Saafi said in her most diplomatic voice. "Family emergency."

"Which doesn't belong in the classroom," Mr. Patel said.

"You're absolutely right, sir." Saafi rose. "We'll take this to the hall." She departed, and Beth followed, nose to her phone.

Mr. Patel's jaw waggled. He cleared his throat to regain his dignity before continuing the lecture. Todd couldn't pay attention, even though he knew the girls would appreciate his taking notes.

Mr. Patel released them to project work, but Todd pushed himself up and followed the girls into the hallway.

"What happened?"

Beth eyed him skeptically. "You don't know?"

"No. What's going on? Where's Claire?"

"Todd, are you really with us now?" For the first time in weeks, Saafi's eyes acquired the haunted look she exhibited around Adam.

"Oh my God, what happened? Is Claire okay?"

Beth and Saafi exchanged a glance before Saafi answered. "She's fine. She'll be here in a couple of hours."

"What happened?"

Beth handed him her phone. "Do you know this guy?"

Todd examined the grainy black-and-white photo, no doubt clipped from security footage. It was Joey.

"Yeah. Adam was trying to partner with him."

"He was arrested early this morning," Saafi said.

"He broke into Maite's place—with a gun," Beth said.

Todd chilled. "Is—"

"Everyone is okay," Saafi said. "Claire lives closest, so Maite called her to help board up the broken windows. She'll update us at lunch, and the police will watch the shop so Maite and her grandma can sleep."

"Shit." Todd pulled at his hair.

"Todd," Beth said, drawing out the single syllable. "You really didn't know?"

"No, I—you think Adam arranged this? No. I know him. He would never..." Never what? Never point a gun at a grandmother in a flower shop? Could Todd say that after Adam had gone after his own half-siblings? After he'd attacked Saafi last year?

Todd and Adam had been pushing boundaries together since they discovered they could outrun Mrs. Thompson, but Adam wasn't just testing the limits anymore. He was crossing lines.

"I swear, I didn't know." Todd barely raised his voice above a whisper.

Saafi looked at Beth. "Do we believe him? You're better at this."

Beth regarded him. "Yeah. We believe him."

Todd didn't have time to appreciate their faith in him. The school secretary summoned him to the office over the intercom.

"Let us know what you learn," Beth said as he departed. Todd nodded, thinking this day would only get worse.

Two familiar police officers greeted him in the hall. Principal Evans ushered them into his office, relinquishing his desk to Officer Quintero as he had before.

Officer Quintero held up a tablet displaying a paused video. She hit play, and the florist's shop appeared. Glass shattered, and two black-clad figures pushed into the store. Todd recognized Adam's form, even with all the weight he'd lost. The other figure must be Joey.

Todd watched, transfixed, as Maite burst into the room, holding a crowbar aloft. Joey pointed his gun at her. Maite dropped the bar and held up her hands, though if eyes shot bullets, both boys would have dropped dead.

Adam strolled around the store, knocking vases off the shelves with a casual air. Maite stepped toward him once, but Joey shook the gun and moved closer. She raised her hands again as Adam poked a piece of glass out the front window.

Though no sound accompanied the footage, Todd imagined the disdain in Adam's voice. He felt no satisfaction watching his brother finally get revenge on the girl they'd always considered a bully. Only the knowledge that Maite emerged unscathed allowed him to continue watching the encounter.

Adam continued to taunt Maite, but when he turned his back, she moved so quickly Todd didn't catch what she did. The gun ended up in her hand, and she elbowed Joey's head so hard he collapsed. Adam reacted too slowly to help his comrade, and Maite aimed the gun at him. Judging by her posture, she knew how to use it.

Either from sheer desperation or wisely calling Maite's bluff, Adam took off through the broken window. Moments later, the two police officers entered the store.

A hundred boulders weighted Todd's chest. In two years, they'd gone from pranksters to pot growers to violent criminals. Todd was struggling to pull himself out of that spiral, but his brother was enjoying the ride.

"I take it the other masked assailant isn't you?" Quintero asked.

Assailant. That's what his twin was now. Todd shook his head, unable to speak.

"Maite said it was your brother, Adam," Officer Johansen said. "Do you know where he is?"

Todd's saliva thickened, and his tongue wouldn't move.

"Time to choose the right path, son," Principal Evans said.

As always, Todd chafed at his use of the word "son," but he couldn't muster his usual sarcastic response. He swallowed thickly.

"What happens if you find him?"

"Ms. Rojas is pressing charges," Quintero said. "Given Adam's age and history of delinquency, he'll probably be charged as an adult."

"You'll put him in jail?" Todd rubbed his stumpy fingers. Adam had always been his hero. Even after everything that had happened, Todd didn't wish jail on his brother.

Officer Johansen cleared his throat. "The judge may place him in a program designed to teach work skills and encourage community reintegration."

"Like, you'd teach him to be a decent human being?"

Quintero smiled. "Something like that."

"That doesn't sound so bad." If Todd could learn, why not Adam? Quintero leaned forward, perhaps sensing she had Todd on the brink. "We need to find him before we can help him, Todd."

Todd glanced at the tablet. What if someone had gotten hurt? If left free, would Adam try again? Would he target their half-siblings next? Todd thought of the happy children in the family photo. He may be ten minutes younger than Adam, but he was definitely their older brother. Was it his job to protect them even if they didn't know he existed?

"Adam has a couple different hangouts." Todd told them to check Old Man Caesar's, a few old girlfriends' basements, and a couple of their favorite smoke spots.

The officers took notes, thanked him, and left. Principal Evans gripped his shoulder.

"You did the right thing, Todd."

"Then why doesn't it feel like it?"

"Who said courage was easy?" He turned to leave and almost crashed into his secretary. She brushed herself off, extra long fingernails trailing over her clothes.

"Your son's school called. I guess he fell off the monkey bars at morning recess. They think you should take him to urgent care, just in case."

"Grady?" Principal Evans's eyes roamed the ceiling as if searching through his memories. He must have come up empty because he shrugged. "Guess he got over his fear of heights. Will you tell anyone who calls I'll get back to them as soon as I can?" The secretary nodded, and Principal Evans waved Todd out of his office.

By the time Todd reintegrated into the school day, he only had one class before lunch, but not even Cathryn's acronyms helped him focus. When he reached the cafeteria, Saafi and Beth were already seated. They looked up when he sat beside them, disappointed expressions revealing they wished he was Claire.

"Did you hear anything else?" Todd asked.

Beth shook her head. "What did they want in the office?"

Todd looked at his hands. He hadn't bothered grabbing a lunch today. His stomach was too stormy to eat.

"I told them where Adam likes to run when he's in trouble."

"Good," Beth said, voice firm. "I know he's your brother, but he pointed a gun at my friend."

"I know. They showed me the security footage." Though Joey had wielded the gun, Adam's behavior had been just as sickening.

"Todd."

Todd jumped at the sharp word. Claire approached the table, looking tired. Tired and angry.

Todd held up his hands. "I swear I didn't know."

Claire looked at Beth, who nodded. "We believe him."

The anger drained from Claire's expression, leaving only exhaustion. She sank into a seat beside Todd, and he restrained himself from wrapping an arm around her.

"How are they?" Saafi said.

"Maite's fffff- fffff- okay, but I've never seen her grandma so scared." Claire eyed Todd's arm, looking like she wanted to use it as a pillow. She rested her chin on her hand instead.

"Go home and sleep," Saafi said. "We'll take notes."

Claire shook her head. "I won't sleep, not after seeing that security footage." She shuddered, and Todd put a stabilizing hand on her back. She didn't lean into it, but she didn't remove it either.

Beth's phone buzzed. "Because today didn't have enough drama."

"What?" Claire said.

Beth rose. "Some idiot tried to push Minh down the stairs."

"Is she okay?" Saafi asked.

Beth waved away their concern. "*She's* fine. The guy she pepper sprayed is not."

"Is pepper spray even allowed in school?" Saafi asked, but Beth was already charging out of the cafeteria to do damage control for her sister.

The three remaining teens sat in an exhausted silence until the bell ended their lunch. The intercom followed, summoning Saafi to the office.

"That's weird," Saafi said. "I don't have any appointments today."

"That is weird," Todd said. "Principal Evans isn't even here. His son's school called. Apparently, the kid fell off the monkey bars, though he's afraid of heights."

"It's Adam," Claire said, her tone serious.

"What?" Saafi said.

"He wants Saafi alone. Think about it." Claire held up a finger for each point. "He attacked the shop, mmmmeaning Maite stayed home. Then he faked an emergency call to get rid of Principal Evans and arranged for B-beth to deal with Minh's situation. He must think I'm ssssstill at Maite's."

Saafi's eyes widened with terror, but Claire grabbed her arm. "I'll go with you."

"Wait," Todd said. "Adam wouldn't come to school knowing the police are looking for him. Even if you're right, why would he call Saafi to the office? Won't there be witnesses?"

"Maybe he's plotting an ambush on the way." Claire's words only made Saafi's shoulders clench.

"Or maybe this is all a coincidence?" Saafi squeaked. The intercom paged her again, and she appeared one more summons away from hyperventilating.

Claire eyed her friend, as if assessing whether her conspiracy theory was doing more harm than good.

"You're right. I'm just t-t-tired from getting up early and jumpy from seeing that video, but just in case, I'll walk you to the office."

"I'll go," Todd said. "You two have your next class together, right? I'll walk you to the office, and Claire can take notes."

Saafi exhaled. "That would be nice. If my grades drop, I might lose my scholarship." Focusing on a mundane academic problem seemed to calm her.

Claire squinted at Todd, but the plan calmed Saafi, so she kept her displeasure to herself. She gave Saafi a fake smile.

"I'll t-take good notes." She whispered in Todd's ear as she passed, "I'll check on Beth. Take care of her."

"We'll be fine," Todd whispered back, though his insides quivered. Something eerie was happening.

Don't be stupid. You're just jumpy after this morning.

As soon as the school secretary spotted them, she rubbed her temples. "I'm sorry, Saafi. Some hooligans hijacked the intercom while I was in the bathroom. You can go back to class."

"Are-are you sure?"

185

The secretary nodded. "Oh, those kids are getting detention for a month if I have my way." She waved them out, and soon her long fingernails were clacking on her keyboard.

Saafi halted when they reached the hallway. "What are the odds that's a coincidence?"

Todd shook his head. "I don't—"

"Todd!" Cathryn sprinted toward them, her skinny legs pumping in a gait as awkward as Minh had alluded to this morning. When she reached them, she put her hands on her knees and gasped for breath. Had this day been less disturbing, Todd would have advised her to spend less time reading and more time exercising.

"What is it, Cathryn?"

"Minh texted me," she wheezed. "It's Claire."

"What?"

"She heard a noise...left to investigate...didn't come back."

"Where is she?"

"Same level as the art room...originally storage...then the old computer lab..."

"I don't need its history. Just tell me how to get there."

Cathryn waved toward the west. "Basement...between the art room...and the old wing."

Todd pushed the sophomore into Saafi's hands. "Stay with Saafi." He caught Saafi's eye. "Stay in the office."

He sprinted through the over-renovated school's twisty halls and leaped down a stairwell. The bowels of the school stretched before him, and the lighting worsened as he reached the older wing. He squinted as he rounded a corner, but he tripped over a broken folding chair. Carpet burned as his elbow broke his fall, and he skidded to a halt.

"Swear you'll stay away from him."

"I'm nnnnot afraid of you."

"I said stay away from him, bitch!"

Todd's stomach churned at Adam's voice. He peered into a nearby room. Two large guys held Claire in front of Adam, but she stomped on one of their insteps and bucked her head into the other's nose. The distraction allowed her to wiggle free, but Adam blocked her escape. The dim lighting glinted off a knife.

Todd raced into the room and tackled his brother. They wrestled for a while before Adam broke free and stood.

Claire grunted. The two guys had recaptured her, and one of them whispered in her ear. Judging by her enraged face, he had nothing appropriate to say. Todd's vision went red. He bowled into the guy like a bull. Scuffling sounded around him, but Todd focused on his target. He pinned the guy to the ground and punched his face. The guy dug his fingernails into Todd's cheek, but Todd batted his hand away and hit him again.

"Stop."

Todd halted, so used to following his twin's commands that he did it without thinking. The guy beneath him groaned, but his eyes remained closed. Todd released his foe when he spotted Adam holding the knife an inch away from Claire's throat. The third guy had pinned her arms behind her back.

"Adam, don't." Todd approached his brother with his hands outstretched. "Don't hurt her."

"She turned you against me."

"You did a g-good enough job of that yourself," Claire said. As much as Todd loved her fire, he wished she'd douse it. She struggled, but Adam pressed the blade against her skin, and she stilled.

"Shut up." Adam's cold calm revealed he knew he was in charge.

"Let her go, Adam." Todd inched closer, brainstorming how to wrest the knife from his brother without hurting Claire.

"She baited you, and you fell for it like another dumb fish." Adam stepped closer, and Claire sucked in a breath. "She'll drop you the moment someone better comes along."

"So what?" Todd's mind spun as Adam turned in surprise. "That's my risk to take." His whole life, he'd let Adam be the brains. Adam made the rules for all their games. Adam planned all their pranks. Adam set up all their double dates, and Adam decided how they'd live after high school. He was done being the loyal little brother, done letting Adam dictate his life just because he'd saved it once. Todd would make his own decisions, even if they hurt.

"You can't choose some chick over your twin." The veins in Adam's neck popped out as he spoke.

Todd shook his head. He'd chosen the greenhouse over the Ides of March, and now he chose courage over loyalty, Claire over Adam.

"Yes, I can."

Adam snarled and pulled the knife back a scant half inch. The small twitch was Todd's only clue to the pending strike, but he reacted fast enough to knock his brother's arm up. His blow sent the knife careening across the room.

Claire wasted no time reengaging in battle with her captor, but Todd couldn't help her. Adam fought like a rabid dog, kicking and flailing at Todd's attempts to pin him. Todd tried not to injure his brother, but Adam offered him no such mercies.

Unable to force Adam to the ground, Todd outmuscled him. He shoved his brother so hard he backpedaled halfway across the room before falling on his butt. Todd raced toward him, but Adam raised his hands in surrender.

"Okay, okay. You win." He shifted into a crouch. "You win."

Todd relaxed his stance, but Adam lurched to his feet, knife again in his hand. A line of fiery pain tore open Todd's triceps as Adam dragged the blade through his arm. Todd screamed, but Adam pulled the knife another inch before yanking it out.

"That was for your own good." Adam pushed Todd aside and stalked to where Claire was losing ground against her opponent. "This is her fault."

Claire's eyes widened, and she tripped over the leg of the guy Todd had defeated.

"No!" Todd dove, ramming Adam's knees and giving Claire a chance to skitter out of her attacker's reach. Adam twisted onto his back, but when Todd tried to pin him, he slashed at his arm with the knife. A crash sounded, but Todd sensed only the second line of pain that crisscrossed the first.

Adam pushed him over. Todd rolled away, but his brother was too quick. Adam straddled him and gripped his injured arm, digging his fingernails into the wound. Todd cried out and tried to knock his hand away, but Adam held the knife over him.

"Traitor," Adam sneered, but something large crashed into his head, pushing him off Todd. He fell face down and didn't move.

"G-guess it's a g-g-good thing old c-c-c-c-computers are sssss- so heavy." Claire gestured to the boxy old monitor she'd hurled at Adam's head. Another lay crushed beside her opponent. Claire exuded a tough-girl air, but Todd guessed her halting speech had more to do with her shaking than her stutter.

"Guess it's a good thing Maite taught you self-defense," Todd said as he struggled to his feet. He pulled Claire into his arms and held her tight. She was trembling so much he felt her heart fluttering against his chest. His own was hammering like a miner on a sugar high.

They held each other in silence while their bodies calmed down from fight mode. Todd's limbs felt heavy, and he had a sudden desire for a nap. A nap and something to numb the pain in his arm.

"Will you go to prom with me?"

Claire leaned back and met his eye. "You're asking me now?"

"If I don't end up in jail."

"They usually don't send the good guys to jail."

Todd hugged her tight, choking on a sudden emotion. "Is that a yes?"

Claire leaned back again, but the dim light shrouded her eyes. She reached behind his head and pulled him into a kiss.

"That's a yes." She patted his chest. "Now let's get you ssstitched up before you bleed to death." One guy groaned. "Or one of them wakes up."

Claire intertwined her fingers with his as she tugged him down the hall, and Todd knew he'd made the right choice.

CHAPTER 30

Between Todd's stitches, the barrage of phone calls, and the mountains of paperwork, an entire day passed before the police, Principal Evans, and the impacted families crowded into the main office. Initially, one woman insisted the "redheaded demon girl" gave "my precious boy" a "severe concussion and emotional trauma," but Principal Evans silenced her by reading the "angel's" enormous file. From then on, the anger flowed only one direction.

Todd sweated in his seat, but Claire squeezed his hand. "Relax. Aunt Monica is a p-paralegal. You won't go to jail."

Todd believed Claire's aunt held some sway over the lawyers she worked for, but he didn't share Claire's confidence that the woman was on his side. Even the police officers kept their distance as she screamed in Principal Evans's face.

"...and another thing. Why the hell do girls need to carry self-defense key chains to feel safe at school?" Beth and Minh's parents nodded, but no one interrupted Monica as she paced around the cramped office. "Give me one good reason why I shouldn't sic an entire firm of lawyers on you."

Principal Evans received the tirade with the calm of a parent corralling an upset toddler and the professionalism of a diplomat negotiating a ceasefire.

"Ma'am, I assure you, we are cooperating with the authorities, and we will resolve this issue promptly. The evidence suggests a single student organized both the harassment toward Minh and the attack on your niece. There is no crime spree at Brooks High. This was one incident."

"It was more than one incident," Todd whispered. No one acknowledged him, but the thought echoed through his head. He looked to where Saafi sat with her father and experienced a disheartening déjà vu. Last year, this office hosted another meeting of angry parents, and he and Adam won the game of he-said she-said. Judging by Saafi's dejected expression, she didn't believe this meeting would bring any more justice than the last one.

"It was more than one incident." Todd stood, and Claire's aunt fell silent. The entire room stared at him. Todd couldn't meet their expectant gazes. He focused on Principal Evans. "Last year, Adam and I said we were just talking to Saafi. We blamed Maite for the fight, but we lied."

Todd had expected a murmur to roll through the crowd, but they stared at him in stony silence. Right. They already knew.

He cleared his throat. "Adam wanted to see Saafi's hair, so we waited until she was alone, and Adam ripped off her scarf, but he didn't stop there. He...he hit her, and...and I helped." He turned to Saafi, and the words he'd restrained all year burst out. "I am so, so sorry."

"Thank you for sharing, Todd." Was that pride in the principal's voice? Todd couldn't tell, but he obeyed when the man gestured for him to return to his seat. "We'll allow the authorities to evaluate both incidents. As for school policy, we'll allow key chain alarms, but tasers, stun guns, knives, tactical pens, pepper spray, and alternative defensive sprays have never been, nor will they ever be, permitted on school grounds." He gave Minh a scolding glare. She raised an unapologetic eyebrow.

"Furthermore," Principal Evans continued, "the basement where this incident occurred was already slated for renovation. As soon as we have the funds, we'll convert it into a shop class, but until then, we will seal it off from students."

The discussion continued for three hours, but Todd leaned his head against the wall and let Claire's handholding counteract the pain pulling at his stitches. He'd done his part. Now the police would decide his fate.

"Todd." Claire nudged him as the parents filed out.

He lifted his head. "I was definitely not sleeping."

Claire smiled. "You were really brave."

"You were the one who flung computers like the Incredible Hulk."

"No, I mmmmeant when you told the truth."

Todd's face heated. "Oh. That was just...I mean..."

"It meant a lot to me," Saafi said. Todd hadn't realized she'd overheard, but her eyes glistened. "I...I didn't realize how much I needed to hear an apology." Her voice rose to a squeak, and tears fell down her cheeks. She wiped them away with a forced chuckle. "So, are we still on for shopping? Falis has quite the game plan."

"Yeah," Todd said. He wanted to do more than apologize, but he couldn't erase the past. He could only make the most of his second chance.

Todd squeezed Claire's hand as he spoke to Saafi. "Could we, uh, add renting a suit to our list?"

Saafi grinned. "Yes, and I know a florist who makes excellent corsages."

Chapter 31

Todd never imagined he'd set foot on the football field again, much less that he'd wear a cap and gown when he did. The spring sun heated the metal folding chairs, and they burned Todd's legs when he sat with the other graduates. He twisted to wave at Claire, whose last name dictated she sit farther back. She grinned and waved back, making the ridiculous cap and gown look good, though not as pretty as the slinky green dress she'd worn to prom.

Prom had been magical. Actually, the dance had been stupid, but spending an entire evening with Claire had been magical. Todd had borrowed the greenhouse truck so he could drive Claire to the lake afterward. She'd laughed when he'd suggested stargazing, saying the cities created too much light pollution. He'd promised to let her show him real stargazing at her grandparents' farm this summer, and she'd pretended to be impressed by the paltry stars visible over the lake.

They'd snuggled in the nest of blankets and pillows Todd had assembled in the truck bed, holding hands and just...existing together. Many guys would consider the date a failure since Claire kept her clothes on, but after two years of drama, Todd wanted something slower, especially if it lasted longer.

Todd blinked out of his reverie. His daydreaming nearly caused him to miss Saafi and Cumar's valedictorian address. He clapped as they finished, thinking that for once someone else needed their hopeful words more than he did.

Many students received their diplomas before him, but he reviewed his mental to-do list for the greenhouse, and soon his row joined the line.

Todd crossed the stage, painfully aware that he was the only Easdon who did. Adam had been sentenced to the program Officer Johansen mentioned. He'd have the opportunity to take the GED at the end. Todd hoped he would.

"Congratulations, son." Principal Evans shook his hand and handed him his diploma. For once, Todd didn't flinch at being called "son." He figured the principal had earned the right to call him whatever he wanted after helping him graduate on time.

Todd found Noah and Mrs. Thompson in the accessible portion of the bleachers. Noah enveloped him in an enormous hug, which Todd returned, not caring who saw. It was time to change his tough-guy image.

"We're so proud of you," Mrs. Thompson said after Noah released him. Her deteriorating stamina had forced her to switch from a walker to a wheelchair. Todd sat between her and Noah, thinking they made an odd family, but one he wouldn't trade for anything.

Todd cheered as Saafi, Beth, Claire, and finally Maite took their turns across the stage. After the rest of the alphabet received their diplomas, the crowd dispersed.

"I'll save you some of Claire's cake," Todd said as he wheeled Mrs. Thompson to the car. She'd insisted on attending the graduation ceremony, but she compromised on the afterparty.

Todd helped her transfer into the passenger seat. Since he lived in her house, he'd insisted on learning to care for her, in case Noah ever got sick himself. It seemed a fitting repayment for the years of free babysitting she'd given his mother.

When she sat safely inside, he folded her wheelchair and popped the trunk.

"Todd?" a man said.

Todd faced him and froze, half-folded wheelchair still in hand. "What do you want?"

His father fidgeted with the ceremony program. "To see you graduate. I'm proud of you, for what it's worth."

"Even thistles bloom eventually." Todd manhandled the wheelchair into the trunk, careful not to crush the baskets that already lay inside. "I don't need your approval. I don't need you, period, so you can stop feeling guilty. Go enjoy the kids you wanted."

"Todd."

The pain in the word drew Todd's full attention.

His father continued. "I know you're eighteen now. Hell, you could file a restraining order against me, but I—" He took a deep breath. "I failed as a father, but I'd like to start over. Man to man. Adam too, whenever he's ready."

Todd shared his father's stocky build and thick blond hair, but it was the emotional turmoil in his eyes that resonated as most familiar. He was begging for a second chance. Could Todd deny him after he himself had needed one?

Todd extended his hand. "I'm Todd Easdon."

His father shook it. "Ryan Easdon."

"You got kids, Ryan?"

He nodded. "Four. Two grew up without me. I'm trying to do better with the little ones."

Todd shut the trunk, buying himself time to think through his next words. "Well, if you want to teach them the value of hard work, our greenhouse just purchased the plot next door. We can always use help watering the plants."

"I'll keep that in mind."

Todd swallowed, sweating more than the spring sunshine warranted. "I live in the house on the property. Drop by any time, though if you want coffee, I know a vegetarian restaurant owner who boasts about her dark roast."

His father hesitated. "I'm more of a barbecue man myself. Perhaps I could invite you over sometime?"

"I'd like that." Todd strode to the driver's side, feeling like a reptile that had shed its eighteen-year-old angst-riddled skin. Now he was shiny and new, ready to conquer the next stage in life.

He dropped Mrs. Thompson and Noah off at the house before driving to the joint graduation party between Claire and her friends. He retrieved the two gift baskets from the trunk and carried them into the community center.

Maite's grandmother fiddled with a bouquet on the banquet table. "There you are. I have your order." She added a small bouquet to each gift basket. "You've planted some extras for me, I hope?"

"Of course."

"Good, because despite all the vandalism, we received hundreds of orders for prom corsages, and now the parents want graduation flowers."

Todd gestured to the grand bouquet before him. "They know quality when they see it."

Ms. Rojas patted him on the shoulder and moved to embrace an elderly white couple Todd recognized from Claire's family photos. Eventually, he'd introduce himself to his girlfriend's grandparents, but he needed to offload his gift baskets first.

Cathryn sat in the corner, nose buried in a book. Figures.

"You always read at parties?"

Cathryn jumped. "I don't attend many parties, and I need to be home by dinner, so…"

Todd held out the heavier gift basket. "This is for you, to thank you for tutoring me. I couldn't have passed my classes without you."

"I get a present?" Cathryn's eyes lit up. She peered into the basket, withdrew a book, and inhaled through its pages.

Todd chuckled. "Most people would sniff the flowers."

Cathryn blushed. "Right. Those are nice too."

Todd cleared his throat. "Listen, this isn't just a thank-you gift. It's an apology. I'm sorry…" *I'm sorry for not helping you deal with your deadbeat dad.* "I'm sorry for bringing trouble to your house. If you need anything, let me know." He hoped she caught the offer for help in the subtext, but she surprised him with a genuine smile.

"Don't worry about it. I won't be living there much longer."

"You're moving?"

"Something like that." She lifted her chin, and her demeanor shifted from bashful to determined. Todd wasn't the only one leaving his childhood behind. Good for her.

Minh wheeled to join them. "Look who survived high school."

"I had my doubts, but a couple of sophomore girls helped me in art." Todd handed her the lighter gift basket. Art pens weighed less than books.

Minh grinned as she withdrew a chocolate bar. "Let me know if you want me to redraw that tattoo, permanently."

"I'm not a huge fan of bunnies. Maybe a thistle?"

"I'll see what I can do." Minh jerked her head at Cathryn. "Come on, let's beat Maite and Saafi at ping-pong."

Cathryn, reluctantly, slid her book into her new basket and headed toward the ping-pong table.

"Minh?" Todd called.

Minh whipped around. "Yeah?"

Todd gestured to Cathryn. "Take care of your friend."

Minh leaned forward, expression menacing. "Always." She pivoted and joined the ping-pong players. They'll be all right.

His burdens unloaded, Todd joined Claire on the loveseat.

Beth eyed him from the opposite chair. "You spoiled my sister. How am I supposed to top that when her birthday comes around?"

Todd shrugged. "Falis and Saafi agreed not to charge me a shoppers' fee if I left a customer testimonial. I'm sure they'd give you the same deal."

Beth snorted. "I'll just beat her butt in ping-pong. That should take her down a peg." She stood. "I'll leave you lovebirds to yourselves."

Claire laughed, and Todd took her hand, enjoying the connection locked in their intertwined fingers. Without his twin, he'd felt untethered. Adam had always been his support, his anchor, but when he'd traveled down a road Todd couldn't follow, Todd learned to stand on his own. He was ready to be someone else's anchor now, if she'd let him.

Todd wrapped his arm around Claire's waist, and she leaned into him. Maybe she'd hurt him, as Adam predicted, or maybe they'd get married and make adorable volleyball-playing babies with red hair and green thumbs. He didn't know what the future held, but he was strong enough to handle it. As for right now, life was perfect.

Curious about Cathryn?

Follow her journey in *The Lies She Wore*

THANK YOU

Thank you for investing your time in *Even Thistles Bloom*. Todd made many mistakes, but I hope he's redeemed himself for you. If you enjoyed my writing, please consider the following:

1. **Leave a review:** Even a two-sentence review is a fantastic way to support an author, and I would greatly appreciate your feedback.

2. **Join my newsletter:** Follow the link or head to my website, cctheworldnerd.com, to subscribe to my monthly newsletter for free eBooks, behind-the-scenes sneak peeks, and other exclusive content.

ABOUT THE AUTHOR

C.C. Hansen has traded Minnesotan mosquitoes for Montanan mountains. When not writing, she either has her nose in a book, her hands in a ball of bread dough, or her feet on a trail through the backcountry.

Find Me Online

- Facebook: https://www.facebook.com/CCHansen3/

- Website: https://ccthewordnerd.com/

ACKNOWLEDGEMENTS

I owe a huge thank you to my beta readers for their invaluable feedback. Many thanks as well to my generous editor, my kick-ass cover designer, and my extraordinarily patient husband. As always, I could not have finished this project without the support of my mom—my sounding board, cheerleader, and therapist rolled into one.